Osiris
with a trombone
across the seam of
insubstance

Julian Semilian

BLACK
WIDOW
PRESS
BOSTON

Black Widow Press is an imprint of Commonwealth Books, Inc.,
Boston, MA. Distributed to the trade by NBN (National Book
Network) throughout North America, Canada, and the U.K. Black
Widow Press and its logo are registered trademarks of Commonwealth
Books, Inc.

Joseph S. Phillips and Susan J. Wood, Ph.D., Publishers
www.blackwidowpress.com

Cover design & text production: Geoff Munsterman
Cover Art: Julian Semilian (juliansemilian.com)
Author Photo: Laura Semilian

ISBN-13: 978-1-7371603-8-0

Printed in the United States of America

To cease to be a ghost with a number in chains,
forever condemned by a faceless master.

Octavio Paz

Osiris with a trombone across
the seam of insubstance

I take a moment here to introduce the somnambulistic circumamblings of a Soul, a Friend in the grips of Forgetfulness, retracing the spiraling motion of a maelstrom, beyond the Horizon of Weeks:

I contracted deciduous nympholepsy from Layson. It never left me—though at times it abated—but kept returning with precise delinquency on a yearly basis and of its own want. Seven years later, under the duress of this illness—for it is our generation's congenital fault that we delight in ourselves as maladies, an inheritance from our great inner currency, the beloved Great Invalid—I wrote the following lines:

> Layson, Layson, dress me up
> In your fire of invisible sleep

I am not one to refuse such gifts but before I go on it is imperative to determine who I am writing to, Thea (sleeping two rooms away, not far enough, till noon as is her wont), or Layson, or both. Thea: a slow angry, poison-producing boiling of fractured and dazed imperatives, a civilization in ruins, out of the march yet still marching, Thea, you are abstractions in marble to constrain your pure impulses, boiling vat of impulse-impaling imprecations: who will reveal to you the secret of nights if not my gritting teeth? Layson: marauder, vertigo, whirlwind, fountain; doubt to society, muse to unusual escapes, reason for being. This (imperative to determine who I am writing to) in order to facilitate the easy circulation along the memory paths, in order to stimulate the traffic of remembering, in order for the longed for comfort of "unbosoming"—Whitman's nomenclature—to occur, in order for the sounding I wish to perform to render the desired result. Because the purpose of this writing is not to make art, in other words to abstract alembic-like a transmuted solution, a poison, stronger or weaker, of what I recall occurred, into the conventions of literature, what I recall occurred in my relationship to Layson, that is, I'm not talking about the re-fashioning of the latest literary style I am entranced with and wish momentarily and perhaps whimsically to emulate and more than likely end up ultimately abandoning on account of it not conforming to I don't know what sort of arbitrary potpourri of criteria of current criticism of private artistic endeavors I might have recently read about in passing. Take for instance the previous "novel" I didn't finish, written as a letter to Thea. In it I was to be sent off as an arcane ambassador on a top-secret mission—a desperate move by the present—to an undiscovered country where the natives make poetry—the ultimate Unknown—manifesting and thus infusing the surroundings with a substance from which new energy sources might be extracted to redeem us out of our current exhaustion. *Can the substance of poetry, once infusing our industry like a surreptitious virus, transmute the constriction of our gestures?* But the fictive element I had set up as my premise had begun to taunt me, the lie to annoy me, despite the pretense of its metaphorical mirror (which I began to despise!) and intruded upon the jagged flow of the personal epistolary style I tried to maintain. I am attaching a remnant here reluctantly, with the caveat that it is no more than a *fragment from an abandoned work*. I did not intend it to be part of the present text. In vain will you look for the "uniting principle". And yes, do not look for me to strain my language skills fruitlessly to indulge your guilty absolutes. I will not dissolve in shame if you do not make out the borderless transitions, the ironic stridulations, if my montage effects do not match your pre-concluded territorial shifts. If I may contrast two mere skies, juxtaposed at random and nearly analogous in your benumbed soup, your blind jello of significances, except perhaps for a very tiny shift in the velocity with which they are played, (we may be dealing here with frontogenesis, and what clouds then, what precipitation!) then so be it. You may take them to be water if you wish, or even layers of decomposing insomnia lining the steep walls of a river of petrified lava in Arkansas. Or simply the expression of an unspeakable exultation, a host of poetical in(s)anities. "Nothing is more irritating than those works which coordinate the luxuriant products of a mind that has focused on just about everything but a system." What if I am merely a captive of my moods? (The shards of a broken cup can't demand matching floor patterns. Or take a wishbone, one side fruitless obliteration, the other wishes fulfilled, strung up together to the same core. The longer fragment grants the wish—thus is worthy—the other is merely discarded, abandoned, from the start filled with the matter of worthlessness. But the two fragments come pre-joined, worth and worthlessness pre-grafted, so that, before the split takes place, caused by the acting out of a superstition, they are inseparable, and no one can tell them apart.) Even to say "abandoned work" is an excuse in case someone with a mania for rigor rummages through the text in search of coruscating seminars of seaming seduction and glimmering rivulets of chaos at the edges of the shifting juxtapositions. Or am I merely chattering in Rorschach while imagining escapades on marauding Escherian boulevards? Whatever I do, the fact remains I remain as always an unmistakable cosmic secretion, a green sap vastly more it than I. A cosmic secretion, that is, whose purposes the present mentality is too restricted to discern. Maybe the siphoning infusion of my abstract whim-strands into the time-space-matter continuum is a contribution you will later be grateful for.

Dear Thea,

I am writing to you from a far-off country.

Here I am, beginning this (what I'm assuming to be for you a) long awaited letter with a quote from Michaux rather than an explanation. Here I am again, you might say, opting for stylistics, gesticulating via quotation, when what I should have addressed first is the issue of the actual distress (I have been imagining) I caused you. An apology for instance for my sudden disappearance. In print I am not a reliable witness, as I opt for the sudden abandon to language landscapes, languescapes that occur as I write. I am filled with fury, with contempt when I think about making an attempt to render via phonemes, alliterations that minuet minutely in abandoned oneiric colonies, vocables cross-dressing for the occasion in fugitive meanings, the prophiled relief of what your mentality might term an event. Events are merely the coagulated refuse of language, as the wise man said. "We must reach for the reflux on the positron level to evade the factor of quotidian spectacle," as he has always declaimed, undetected in a kaleidoscope of shifting podiums. Because even to skin an event in attempt to make out its imprecise intestines and expose them on rostrums of praise or contempt is straight-jacketing I don't condone, pre-established quartering of the infinite. I almost wrote gartering of the infinite. Why regiment my writing fingers into infantile ankylosis through the offices of meaning? Newsmen, journalists, autobiographists, all terrorists out to jackhammer the chalcedony of the imaginal with their pre-ordained arrangements. And you, salivating under the moon over their reptile skits. Of course the thought of you still entrances me, don't think it doesn't, still does, months later, how could it not, but for that I despise you. Who gains from it? The body of legislated flesh forced to march to the reduced drum beat of word concatenations, sent out and then brought back all chained together, only to force us into the boots of the march.

I will address this issue of my disappearance in due time—as I remain perusing into the haze and howling at the unspeaking horizon from my promontories of distress. You will call me a Maldoror of appropriating stylistics at the most inappropriate of times. You may determine that I am exercising a form of cruel magic to reciprocate for all your various diseased progressions by delaying what should be clear to me you wish to know first. In fact I may not even be writing you from a far away country. Perhaps, like a present day Wakefield, I may be present, hovering closer than you suspect. My stylistics are rooted in undulating snakes, in whose service we are engaged, whose purposes none of us may grasp. I once wrote, I recall, never a member of the colonizing force, I undulate among the voracious nations of history. Still, you'll be surprised, I have taken to deconstructing myself because what good is style, you'd ask, when say, six thousand people are eviscerated "in one fell swoop", so to speak, and you know how I hate manners of speech. What good is style, you'd ask, to someone who loses one madly loved, say. But me, kill them all, I still crave the quicksand seduction of my glossolalia, my echoing oneiric colonies. I drink my self-formulated aphrodisiacs in labyrinths where I am stalked and about to be ambushed by delirious words bedighted as erotic beings of light waiting to abduct me in order to bend me to their purposes. Then I lend myself to their unrestricted whirlpool of pleasant poison, I live for the promise of their coruscating seminars, while outwardly raging against the utterings of a Friend—lingering malignantly in my formulations from the previous century—who upbraids me by translating a Neruda at his most Stalinist insidious, declaiming on a proletarian rostrum before the adoring mass of salivating disciples slobbering over his luminous adjectives, that this is not the time for oneiric labyrinths. His luminous adjectives, on an Eros defrocking patrol. That this march, dissolving into the sleeplessness of historical statues—sleeplessness not wakefulness—is the march of time and to be out of step with this march is to be out of step with the march of life, you will only be left behind in a pile of refuse in the junkyard of a filthy cockroach infested tenement, worse, your heart frozen even to laughter, "treading the traffic of futile roads," while the singing brother-marchers in arm-in-arm formation melt forth into the horizon of his luminous adjectives. I may be the first to declare that I dissolve in shame at the immodest declarations of his declamations. This tyrant of benign compulsion, entreating you to march with fists high in the air rather than roam with them stuffed complacently into the torn pockets of an ideal coat, gaze set forth into a pre-concluded horizon rather than sitting under the stars by the side of the road amidst the fantastic shadows. "Enough roaming," he says, "enough torn pockets and ideal coats, enough fantastic shadows and partial moons perused through the clouds, we are marching in favor of the cloudless model, heroically photographed by the light of our much sung about morning sun." I wept more than all the children in the world, cornered like that into military styles of poetry, threatened with the tin can strewn attic, left merely to tongue a single word, nay, a mere vocable, stuttering on a vocation-less vocable, my baroque viola of spit and stuttering. This sal(i)vador thus having charged his slobberers with ammunition to taunt me with retarded rhetoric about the delight of bathing in the sweat of the common man raising his fist in favor of gaining the constitutional right to beat his dreams into flesh. I return the favor and give these Procrustean Maldorors a Neruda in the mirror salivating over the mystery of his own legs:

> For a while now I've been standing
> staring at my legs,
> With my never-ending and curious longing,
> with my vehement zeal
> As though they might have been the divine
> legs of a diabolical empress
> abducted inside the abyss
> the ocean
> as though I were suddenly
> despite my purpose

soldered to the void
as though giving free reign
to my supreme desires,
standing on the threshold of disappearance,
of dying of not dying

As I said, I know you are curious to know what, what I mean is I am being euphemistical when I say curious, I am impertinent, to keep what I am assuming you are dying to know away from you for so long, risking that "perilous chasm in human affections", while indulging once again in my baroque phantasies and lavishing in labyrinths of language. But I already said this. Even to say dying to know is such an imprecise figure of speech and I am suddenly stuttering in identifying myself as its utterer. But the indulgence of these words that incarnate as I utter them insists, as my moist long tongue fashions them as fetish, phoneme by phoneme, quantum sound integer by integer sound quantum, consonants consorting in labile entrancement in the ooze mother of vowels of entrancement and abandon. This language I fashioned of my insomnia, these words I made of rats and irrational dentures, scurrying across the floors of sleepwalking, this language I fashioned for you out my murdered renunciations. It is only this that I long for and I know it is on its account that you accused me of needing no one except for the occasional abandon to the call of the catalogue you and I spoke of indulging in on many occasions—and suddenly I find myself grasping for you as I indulge and pause, abducted inside a memorious catacomb, my tongue now a maddened Bartok of the quartets indulging in your labile ooze, a languorous soldier commanded to the cause of erecting you statuesque to the plinth of the much fabled volcanic explosion you claim you have so far been denied. I darkly scanned across the length of my suspended clauses and bemoaned the severe lack of a multitude of the letter 'l', letter 'l' is soft like a vowel, l, liquid pleroma enveloping you like a willing bilingual lover lapping at your shore, l is tongue and spit, the way you suck in so that the top tip of the tongue licks the top tip of the palate behind the teeth, sticking thus wet to wet, soft to hard, hard to soft, I will scorn you if you do not continue to read, lake, littoral, saliva, lassitude, labia, languorous clitoric indulgence, literature that I long and long long for. Do I crave to make literature? And, to reiterate, at a time like this? No, no, I tell myself, I protest, and risk missing the deadline to take me to the message-bearer whose duty it is to make the drop of my words at the next assigned interstice in the minutely pre-programmed network of illicit postal stations leading eventually to the anxious grip of your slender fingers. (Your fingers' winglets, I assume, will palpitate about the letter like the tracery buzzing of transparent nerves, disordering the winds of your formulations.)

Yes, this is a letter and I am writing it only to you. To you whom I abhor, to you whose system of malfunctioning formulations is everything I have staked my life's purpose against and the reason I left. I am writing it now, I am transmuting thoughts into words now before your eyes, but have been fashioning and re-fashioning the sequence of these words before transmuting them to words on the page, with thoughts—which are fish of wind, blood marinated windfish that writhe in the blistering blood-bath inside my seabrain—blood-stained airfish for you—this letter being my explanation to you, the exploration of my disappearance, every unrecorded instance slipping between the transparent membranes of well-fashioned thought. Some writers claim to hammer the shape of their phonemes into sentences for the amorphous masses, these phonemes phashioning the so-called words which they wave like standards, words to which they attach mothering significances, words which they claim are the mothers of the masses, claiming them to be the jai alai for the hoi polloi, shameless pre-programmed prevaricators! perpetrating the standard of their "love for the common man" agenda. Their appeal to an audience's parlor marching boots, didactics that frighten my intestines into suddenly exuding essences that churn against the state of my well-being. Because anytime anyone waves the standard of the "masses" along with their intestinal march, I would force them before the psychic dentist and wrench out howling and flailing in vile protestation some grotesquely shaped minus they've varnished in the veneer of their ethical turmoils, theoretical ax-murderers on the march. (But who is the writer who does not imagine his reader? And one is ashamed admit it, who the reader one imagines is.) But writers, you know how they are, you spotted it right away, in one of your few moments of sharpened lucidity, they can say anything to the masses that indulge in salivation over the enigma of their bon mots. As for me, I am writing this letter only for you. I am writing to you and for you alone because my sudden disappearance must have distressed you to the core and I assume you wish to hear from me. There is no artistic intent in this, this is by no means literature. This is a letter, meant only for you. And this is not art for art's sake, so abhorrent to my Friend and his throng of tumultuous salivators, this is simply a letter with a purpose, its purpose being to explain to you what you want to know, what has happened to me. A listing of events. As abhorrent as event listing is to me. As I said, I am sorry to have caused you so much distress. Maybe I didn't say it, but I am sorry. The thought of the agony I assume you must have felt as the days wore on and you eventually concluded I would never return has been stirring me to involuntary self-denunciation. This despite the fact, let it be known, I have long and publicly abrogated, more, on self-propelled rostrums denounced self-denunciation and its disabling and disabled discipling followers. You don't know this about me but I had in past times, among other things my entranced public worshipped me for, led mass marches demanding the abdication of remorse. But I've been fabricating for you—and when I say, write fabricating, what a teeming I see, an engendering—phonemes, vocables elegantly strewn into phashioned significances, but this is the first time I have given myself to anchoring their passage to the page, despite themselves. An event whose tessitura I don't know I know how to speak of, after all what is the difference. And yet I pause to speak of it. And if I say I can't speak of it, I perceive it, I perceive the stream—a stream creeping spider-like through the network of pipes that crisscrosses the entire unknowing width of the wordless amorphous, coagulating into impalpable brief significances—the stream of the transition yet my heart remains mute and resistant to interrogation. The words that were to be interrogated now refuse to render meanings. I should have obeyed the advice of a friend, I must not question my words' intent too intently if I do not wish them to become meaningless, to scurry around amoeba-like in a purposeless vat. I was looking perhaps for a transmutation of substances with no names, streams, there was perhaps a change in purpose, from thoughts to words, the desire perhaps, absurd to think I should have thought, thought not written, thought against written, I must push on, the anxious call of the narrative, though I must warn I cannot be certain this letter will reach you. It is to be smuggled out of here, the letter, not yet finished, via an intricate and complex network of routes and rouses, as I mentioned, whose details I cannot reveal to you for fear it may fall into the fingers and before the miscomprehending perusal of some who wish to prevent it from getting to you. Please destroy it as soon as you've read it. Know that more than likely you are being watched, though I cannot tell you who it is who's watching you. Do not trust anyone. There are neither good guys nor bad guys anymore. THERE ARE ONLY COMPLEXES OF AGENDAS IN SERVICE OF MOTIVES NONE OF US CAN COMPREHEND. A great plot is being perpetrated and we cannot prevent it. An invasive poison is adumbrating our clairvoyant Speech and we're left stuttering helplessly but cackling nonetheless. We do not even know who the opposing forces are and who works for what side. All that remains for us is to posture for an imagined good, an unexamined emotional stance to sustain our need to alleviate our troubled conscience. Please sustain yourself with the conviction that the memory of you still entrances me. I know I should have bowed momentarily for your sake to your beloved form of convention and said I still love you. But love, I fear (the word love, I mean), is always to be used for its short-hand dramatic effect. I don't even know who is in charge of love anymore, or in whose service it is used. There are no more standard bearers for it, neither Bretons, nor

Lautreamonts, neither de Sades nor Sacher-Masochs. And the word itself, love, has long lost its consistency, has been used up by those who sell its accoutrements, those who are always bedecking our decomposing skeletons in new amorous allures in order to sustain these habit formations, this decomposing march. Short of a miracle, I don't know that I will ever see you again. Even if a miracle should occur, how do we know who caused it? The breath of fresh air still cools brow, but not thought, such are the times we live in. No more "the summer bedrooms where you delight in becoming one with the soft night." No more "The days and nights when despite all I was still calm." And in the shadows, who splits the profits?

I am writing to you from a far off land. A virgin nymph named Shuzo Takiguchi flits by. "The air is a beautiful princess without bones," she moans, wrapped in a nude wind.

☿

As I said, I only want, my only purpose here, and hold me to it please, is to delve into the past's reservoirs, make my memory speak, so to speak. The cauldrons of memory to render their secreted effect. You may be surprised I say "hold me to it". You may be surprised, that is, if you're not merely skipping through the text, or if your attention is not glued to every word before you merely because you may feel obligated to me—and it is possible you may—to read what I write—and then it would only be appropriate to say "trudging" through the text—or perhaps even because I am read by unknowns for reasons of national security in hope of finding the clues they're looking for—because more than likely they are aware of my thoughts, while my whirlwinds of pleasant poison can do nothing if not arouse suspicion— and though I have been for the most part outwardly silent, expressing myself in public places—in expressing what needs to be said, when the subject came up—merely by a slight ironical upturn of the left corner joining my upper and lower lips, though at times balancing it with the same motion to the right—a conscious act I performed, committed, for reasons right now too numerous to enumerate, such as simply to balance, on account of my secret need—a need I mainly disdain—to be symmetrical, my disguised obsession with symmetry! So many convolutions I have forced my formulations to perform in order to satisfy this obsession with symmetry, and then to simply obscure my obsession with symmetry via convolutions I have performed as though via an obsession I may have picked up like a virus to emulate my intestines. Or because I suspected at times that even the subtlest of gestures you perform or commit yourself to, by the use of exterior body parts, such as sections of your face, have an indelible, inexorable effect on your internal organs, this idea perhaps having forged passageways into my formulations through partial incomprehension and incomplete absorption of ancient Chinese belief systems whose texts I have perused in passing—while chewing absentmindedly a crunchy Breton cracker doused in liver pâté—thus, I am saying, by not balancing you may be exercising, say, your liver or your, say, kidneys or intestines—which are certainly very important to exercise, I am by no means undervaluing the need to exercise them—but not your, say, heart, which I think perhaps is even more important, or your liver and so on, so you can, in fact, never overemphasize one side in favor of another, or rather, overemphasize both sides, that's what I meant—thus, it is not possible that my viral internal demeanor has not been, if not spotted or detected (this despite the fact that the fragrance of night and the fast wind of dreams push through the air at far greater speeds), at the very least suspected. Notice was taken, I am certain, and eyebrows raised in consternation, when I made the fugitive but haunting allusion—with my indicative, Whitmanesque arm—in a certain public place, riffling gracefully through a spectrum of undecodable vocables, about becoming the cause of the "illness's illness". I was speaking of the present, of course. So if you did notice, I say "hold me to it" because the pressure is there to give an account of what I am about, both in artistic circles and outside, and when I say artistic circles, I mean both those I belong to and those I don't and despise because they are—despite the name—nothing but fuel for the maintenance of the present.

I am saying that even these words that I string along in the silence of my private demesne are to be waded through by the self-appointed pundits of *public* opinion and placed on pedestals of *public* display in order that their content be thoroughly examined and if necessary, constrained, along with their secretor. My words are waded through by the self-appointed pundits of *public* opinion whose secret missions are to provide data for military philologists, hordes of army philologists armed to the teeth with interpretations. Because my personal contribution to the *public* discourse, no matter how private, is inimical and in opposition, purposefully so perhaps—the perhaps remains for purposes you might or not discern—to the present and the present manner of presenting matters before the *public*, and thus inserting myself in the *public* mix in such a viral manner that it and I must be thwarted like the start of a vicious contamination. Such a pernicious internal voice must instantly be throttled, be relegated to the refuse of cultural contempt, must be run through the thresh of devaluation, and its conductor too refused, even eliminated, on grounds of national security, my heart declared a source of *public horror*, a toppler of the present in potentio and its reservoirs of voices frozen. Yes, I am speaking here, I am listing the various functions of the factories that manufacture cultural contempt, which are engaged to work *overtime* nowadays, and not just them but the covens and coteries that have been engaged or even proudly engage themselves day and night, knowingly or unwittingly, knowingly and unwittingly— this is the frightening truth—like newly converted marionettes, as spokespeople unwittingly trumpeting truths they are imbibed with surreptitiously by these factories that manufacture cultural contempt. Thus, the *public opinion*, the most feared of fanfaronades. In such a climate I fear, it is clear, I am not perceived by the present as one of its valuable assets. *Public opinion*, engaged without pay, I would say (because so many crave the rostrum, and don't care who writes their discourse, they simply select the first discourse they spot in their general fumbling about through the *public* discourse, mantled in the constrained drag of the *mirrored gesture they crave*), by the forces of devaluation with which it joins voluntary hands, an onrush of rivers of joining of voluntary hands, of those who for the most part are capable of nothing but "dumb shows and noise", *public opinion* which could be counted at times, in times now long past, to be kind, surprisingly so but yes, public opinion which surprisingly appeared at times infused with revolutionary aromas, bedighted even and mirroring itself perfumed for glimmering moments in revolutionary intimacies, enjoining even to join the underground, *public opinion* which at times, rare to be sure, infused you with the comforting illusion of straining towards the mild and popular versions of the imponderable, mild yes, popular yes, but still. A small comfort. Why not. An indulgence to be sure, a small comfort zone, like a half-tone portrait of bilious Baudelaire on a tin of bitter liqueur bonbons, no more, but still. "The unskillful laugh, the judicious grieve." So there is nothing left of unbosoming, unbosoming good bye, (Whitman your dream turns to nightmare, it's all forced confessions from here on, Walt! What do you see Walt Whitman, where are you, are you still here with me? I am not too sure. You are not too sure either. Are you reconsidering, Walt? Let us talk of death, oh you lover of lovers who taught me to fling my head back as though the region of the unfathomable were my amorous parade!), good-bye unbosoming, except to those who spigot your memories to reservoirs of public humiliation and devaluation, to the torturing of... but no more now and more to come.

As to the matter of expressing myself merely by the slight ironical upturn of the corner of my joining lips, which I mentioned above, it is not so far back in the text but I bring it up again so as not to force you to return to the previous lines up the page, or in the previous page, I don't know how these will turn up eventually in print—yes, I do have print phantasies, why not—thus, regarding the slight ironical upturn of the left corner of my joining lips, don't think I have not incessantly perplexed myself with questions as to the efficacy of my subtle protests on the national front, don't think I have not incessantly plagued myself with questions as to my stance on the national arena, the international even. Questions of exploding poets. Perhaps this is the time of to-morrow's exploding poets that poet made mention of, with perhaps a tinge of bile. An explosion *might* be about to occur, alchemically incited by my secret acts— many of which I might weave parenthetically into the text to follow—summoned as they are, summoned, by an arcane and unheard of until now tyrannical and explosive wisdom. Whose messenger I may be. It might be too late now for anyone to thwart it. Or even me.

☿

All this in defense of my taking up so much of the text on the page to paint myself in such inconclusive features, contrasting this fugitive portrait of myself— kowtowing as I appear to be to realms of senselessness and incomprehension, to a subterranean cartel of a thought that repeats itself 44 times—against the century's historical statues to theoretical ax-murderers, why would they not build a statue to my pursing lips? Or my flung-back head?

Behind time and its typewriter teeth there is nothing, absolutely nothing, I'm surrounded by death.

Of course when I say make my memory speak I am being abstract, general. I am perhaps using expressions, manners of speech, words, strings of words concatenated, concatenated in order to be forced into generally accepted meanings, and concatenated so by others. Words which the contempt and praise promoting factories have programmed in the voluntary mouths of the above mentioned public opinion pundits. The underground too—which is generally taken to symbolize the workings of the Id, the involuntary workings of the Id—has now been fitted with rails and trains run through it. Such has been claimed. But perhaps it is only a matter of personal defeat, bile raised to the level—mistakenly so—of the march of time. But if I were to investigate further I would never go on. Still. To go on. There are in my estimation subterranean pathways, *unterwegs*, a reticulary traffic of word-ferrying thoughts, or thought-ferrying words, or perhaps ideas, I don't know exactly which at the moment, definitions are unclear to me at the present moment, winter mornings are generally difficult for me and everyone else is also vague on the matter, assuming you know what they mean when they speak of such things, while I am essentially a partial philosopher, one ridiculed (even by my own self!) for missing the reliable system, and to confess, I never took the time to get one, a system, and though I might glow as an intransigent dispatcher in discourse, I mostly rely on sudden perceptions, unreliable—but who can protest, and how—or maybe reliable, yes reliable, that choose to regale me at the most inappropriate of times with appropriating me as their receptor and reporter and then the reticulary traffic appears in a light slightly sharper than the vague and then I reach out of my mantle of forgetfulness with my imprecise arm, fashioned too of forgetfulness, for the reach for the for the... *and it's mostly gone and the best I can do to console myself is the imaginal brush of a longed for, because it is something that we forgot and that though it is in the nature of sloth and divinity to embrace forgetting like a burgundy curtain that falls endlessly over our doing, forgetting is also a defiance, a concealing before whose force we are helpless—perhaps begging or at least praying might be appropriate here, an outright worship before the Gates of Forgetting*—notice I am not speaking of forgetfulness, but of Forgetting itself, like a cross fade into nothingness, into a conniving nothingness however, a pouch made of a material we don't comprehend, a pouch into which we are not allowed to peer, a pouch redefining peering for you or redefining you for peering, or peering redefining you, but I can't don't want to speak about that now, will speak of it later perhaps, don't be surprised if it pops up in this text again, I was speaking of subterranean pathways, *unterwegs*, a reticulary traffic of word-ferrying thoughts, or thought-ferrying words, or perhaps ideas whose routes need to be detected precisely in order for one to report precisely on their activities. Because there are activities occurring of their own want which are not reported to the general public, certainly ignored by the public opinion. This I can attest to. Activities which the general public ignores, is made to ignore, possibly forced to ignore on purpose, I can attest to that, and which we ignore as well in attempting to forge, or force, or forget, for ourselves, a dimension of living, of gesticulating and comfort, gesticulating and comfort I spoke of before, of gesticulating in comfort, floccinating I would venture—make sure you look it up in the Oxford—apart from these activities. I mention these activities because we ignore them, because we have been herded into a march fashioned of forced habit formations, of obligatory common activity, we have been herded in order that we engage our life force to function in service of present modes of purposeful forgetfulness. In service of the present, which I abhor. (I am speaking of course of the general present, not the one extolled by the pundits of mindfulness.) *A form of, I dare say, current slavery*, let it be said with the force of conviction—come Walt Whitman, what does your Song of Occupations say now? It is perhaps time for the Song of Pre-Occupations—but if I said it, I would more than certainly not be interviewed on television on any of the current popular shows, in order to enter the national discourse, if you get the larger meaning of what I am saying. I must speak via circuitous routes, routes I have long and lonely traveled, mental traveler, not the no-longer existent long brown path seeking, seeking I don't know what sort of recompense, a recompense I now seek in words alone—and what god beseech for them, what heaven—these words which when uttered, or written, are uttered or written without the least hope of being heard (except for the moon who took a liking to me. And like the man said, it has always been the fashion to talk about the moon. And you, Thea, Thea and Layson both, who have complained that I only take you to the border of imprecision and not beyond into the imponderable, that I merely fabricate these clouds of imprecision, a mere coruscating adagio for intestinal strings.) But if I must speak by circuitous routes it is because, well, there is no need to explain it now, is there? The illness has reached alarming proportions—the national discourse must be entered by the back door—proportions beyond measure, proportions whose dimensions, if I were to pause to consider, to pause to measure, are of a magnitude that frightens my inner formulations, diminishes them, while the reticulant traffic of words ferrying thought and idea, I am being imprecise here, as I too am not allowed entry, I am prevented at the entrance, you will spot me incessantly flailing at the entrance, but I do it with a purpose, because I suspect that from these activities perhaps new and dynamic sources of energy may be drawn in the future. So it is not all hopeless, as I had sentenced myself to be a few sentences behind, I confess, confess, that I am hopeful, a statement which will surprise most of you. Yes, many of you will be surprised by my statements. And I do hope to enter the national discourse. From there it's just one step to the international.

☿

A few days ago, a month maybe, but who's counting, I wrote the following, which you should peruse yourself against: "Thoughts are words—have you thought that thoughts are words? Think, thoughts, thoughts, thoughts, what do you see? Thoughts are gigantic worms that pass into procession from the unregarded horizon of through-your-brain procreation, chains of them, concatenated to one another in a never-ending intestinal historical parade, and we are in the tribunes like the state apparatus in the reviewing stand—watching, cheering, not dying. And it is clear where a worm ends and the next one begins. Most of the time it is clear, as worms are clearly defined. I do not even have to say how they are defined because you see them. You say worm, you do not say worm and a quarter, worm and a third. Because worms were manufactured such by someone whose purposes we know nothing about. Who does the wormmaker work for? Go against the general wormmaker. But I protest! See for instance, half of the present worm and half of the next worm, the purple and the cobalt blue, the kermes, a stunning cross fade from one to the other as you stroll your perusal, a correspondence such as never before, as they complete one singular thought. Take a quarter of the present worm and three quarters, even two thirds of the next. What exactly makes a complete worm anyway? Whose meaning is it? Who's measuring three quarters or halves or thirds. I won't venture into smaller or less definite units, I leave that for you, I am loath to delve into counting, I am fearful of math sort of things, perhaps this is a lack on my part, but I can't hold them for long in my head, the present's illness, but don't think that they aren't. How do you define units, integers, completenesses, sine-qua-nons? Are they coming from the future and disappearing into the past? Are they coming from the past and we must follow them in the future to be "in-the-know"? In whose service are they such? Whose purposes define, defile them?

These are the news from around here, though no newspaper will pick it up.

To delve into these activities must be our only goal. We have been conducting our daily march, have been straight-jacketed, I should say, into our daily march by imperception of our resources. The stomach growled and we followed cluelessly, our path to forgetfulness, cuelessly groping in the dark, discovering nothing by our daily floccination, and thus the march of history, no more than a science of carphology. The blind leading the blind. I hate to observe myself resorting to the commonplace, but there you have it. In blind forgetfulness we marched to the dictates of the stomach, not that I am speaking badly about my intestines, they are fine where they are, and I am sure they are doing a fine job, unaware that the energy sources lie elsewhere, not the intestines, but we, forgetful of the elsewhere lying energy sources. Instead we deploy and thus deplete unreplaceable amounts of our internal energy to deploy the external energy necessary to maintain our social masquerade. This is history. Why are we so intent on keeping up the social masquerade, why do we deploy the meager remains of our psychic energy to power up this vicious marionette? To protect perhaps and keep in place the catalogued non-discoveries of the ancients and flailing and floccinating about through the fog for clear and kind counsel and solace to their fright. Our fright now.

☿

Yes, we have created the industrial revolution under the deluded notion of designifying the iguana (I mean Lorca's iguana that bites those who don't dream.) This signified progress. How could we have been so hare-brained? Thinking like rabbits in the jaws of the giant iguana herself. How could we have allowed them to take control?

☿

But we must halt our critique of our insufficiencies in order to pursue the activities that are calling to us to delve into. The reticular venation of the catacomb's couloirs. To molest intestinal graves of grammar left unmolested.

☿

There is however a wall I need to break through, it is not just them preventing via imposed forgetfulness, though that has a lot to do with it, I am exhausted from banging my fists and railing against it, or rather a magnetic force that occurs which attempts to prevent me from exploring beyond the promontory on which I find myself, this malefic, magnetic force drawing me to the center of a dark desire, a maelstrom of, a dark downward spiraling vortex leading to a tarry coagulation that speculates by refusal alone, whose function is refusal alone, whose nature, essential nature is refusal, its own refusal, empire of refusal, or rather refusality, is its essential attribute, its refusality is an integer, of absolute intransigence, or so it seems; and masticates all light that might break through, even vague, and turns it into tar. Can you consume light to where it is no longer, or merely imprison it and thus conceal it? It was of you, Layson, I wanted to speak but it is only me that I am speaking of. Perhaps I should not write these words to you, these words which I now set on the liquid screen of my iBook by pressing the keyboard with letters on my iBook, these oaring barks to the untarred, like attempting to resolve cryptograms posed by the patterns of the void, these words which I suspect will surprise me once I can fly away heron-like from this promontory of distress, or perhaps I should write it to Thea, to you Thea about Layson, unbosoming all to you as though I were writing to you but not quite daring to tell it all to you, for fear of your customary bile spewing, this yellow bile restriction whose coagulation resulted in the civilization whose discomfort we endure, whose discontents we are. Speaking of intestines, I had written to you: *The yellowish goo of the six eggs you ate raw in order to spite me leaked down to your thin intestines, tortuous routes to the mysteries of your stomach churning to make what you are, but for reasons I can't discern right now I didn't think of them as tortuous, I didn't even think about your intestines but of a vague amorphous inside which I considered only in terms of the exterior, your well-toned and taut abdomen, like the known and the unknown, the known which now I crave to place my palm on, to brush the tips of my fingers over, because even, say, doctors whose business is to slice open stomachs with their all too acuminate tools and personally eyeball, unbatting an eyelash, intestines at first-hand, if those doctors were placed in a posture to inspect your well-toned and taut abdomen—and I have seen those doctors! I have met them!—I doubt they would for an instant think about the tortuous path of your intestines, let alone I, not a trained scientist, no, I am a scientist! a scientist of the undefined, a scientist of the unfinished, of the amorphous, of the indefinite, the untermed, a scientist of fog, a scientist of the unspeakable, though there is no such rubric in the social register, there's no "Who's Who" for the scientist of the ineffable, I who vaguely know, know! know is nothing but a memory membrane, thin like a pair of stockings, of interior of stomachs from pictures I saw long ago, and wouldn't it be a profitable idea, a line of stockings called "Diaphanous Memories", sold of course at Pictoria's Intrigues, in whose fabric is woven the painted convolutions of intestines, the memories of your memories of painted intestines you saw in your high school anatomy manual—o knowledge, so tenuous you are, so ephemeral and diaphanous—and oh to drown in the delicate cool mist of your thin intestines braided like fainting spells around my thighs my soles my ankles my knees, o to rush to rush my naked heart against them! because you're my stockings, what are they but the flagrant breath of transmuted intestines, a gift from the unsuspected, a diamante flecked solution to elicit forgetfulness and vertigo, yes what if we used our intestines for stockings? We'd have to stretch them out but*

I am sure they'd give, I am sure they are elastic enough. My sartorius, I suddenly paused and heard myself voice, when you breathe on me these Mysteries of Nothing, my dreams, my fluttering ideas, my failure in eternity, my thirst for myself, it thrills and frills me to unreason. Skeleton vested in a new enamored skin, I was suddenly soldered to the void, attempting to peer over the parapet, a plunging soldier of vertigo, of fainting spells. My intestines, I shouted from below—though they were yours—imprecise chimeras, are my singular list of assets. Oh the murmur, these vast, candid intestines! Why should I be ashamed? I sing now for you my coruscating adagio for intestinal strings:

> Your intestines are a moonless chalcedony sky
> ambrosial mist of terrified disciples,
> and I fear I will swoon
> before I gain the river of night.

The good of the earth has filtered through the labor of the ages. And they are warm and comforting like a womb, we might as well succumb to their perishing delight, their ensconsing perdition. Wet and warm, why worry so much about appearance anyway? The material fashioned directly from the steam and fabric of the universe without the stamp of industry. Our appearance is pure theatricality upon which we bestow even more theatricality. We are sophisticated by deceit.

☿

who could touch that misty mucilaginous terrain of the in-between? That city of vortex and enigma? That convex blur of swoon and transcendence? That dazzle of implied luminance, solar strand streaking, forming edge of this edge? Here I am, terrified that I fumble in the undefinable, I am a mere mud traveler attempting to decipher the Mysteries of Magnification with the spokes of a discarded black umbrella. May I allow myself to press on, peddling this, paddling in *this vociferous goo in hope of happening upon the tail of a recognizable rainbow, or the indicative dove, or simply reassign myself to the safety of the modest pension of the quotidian narrative, while attempting a stolen glance over the parapet into the baroque fold of Deleuze and the delusion of erotica. I will cause revolutions of the imagination! I wished to shout as I carped at the pool of indissolute inconstancies I craved, pooling for them to coagulate on the plinth of recognition I wished to enshrine them on before terror or torpor overtook me and I longed to drown. But why should I perpetually bow to vows made by others, why should I contort my reflection—no matter how minimally—to reach accord, what if I should wish, I reflected in imitation of the absurd, to bow to pirates of sugar confronting armadas of cauliflower? Of eggplant? Oh absurd, absurd Julian! Confronting the cruel mundo with your ice-cream missiles! And so kept staring at your well-toned abdomen and wondering what all those six eggs may have done to your fine thin shape, and further inquired into the state of your thin intestines, your thin intestines by extension, say, splattered in a junkyard on a cloudy day with a background of discarded automobiles and pipes, steamy intestines which to a rambling dog pack might be dinner; mere dinner; how little does this matter to dogs, the labyrinth intricatecies of my yearnings furrowing out from you, the convolution of your intestines worms for culture lack dogs, your stockings the steam of intestines a meal for culture-lack dogs, what is life thought I then but theatrical intestines, a single-time source of meal for dogs while for me the eating still goes on. Yet you are there, I know it, these words now between your thin fingers, this coruscating adagio I have written for your intestinal strings, intestines intact for the duration, a duration hurling upwards against their decomposition, perhaps "the force that through the green fuse drives the flower," duration right now that I know apart from you imbricated in the form-fitting steam of my thoughts of you now inquiring on their own why they, the eggs, did nothing, nothing at all to alter your taut very well-toned form and the gold of the goo insisted vaguely in the background, amalgamating with your nausea and mine from eating the six eggs, yours from eating them, mine from thinking about your nausea, you had asked me how many eggs had I used and I said six and I was so agitated at your report of discomfort, because the erotica amalgamated sadly with your discomfort, though you said you felt discomfort I couldn't, in frustration at these impassable borders, ascertain the dimensions of your discomfort and finally made myself a cheese sandwich which was all we had left in the refrigerator. Cheese here of course beholden to no symbolism. Free to pose no issues. Can be snuck in-between and no one would notice. Perhaps a sense of ennui parading in beige but for much less. Not to explore. Valueless in the narrative. I can't go on, I must go on. A constricting horizon. A disobedient event in its insistence on its own valuelessness in the narrative. Not a point through which a welcome blue lake begins. Can we ever ascertain then the dimensions of anyone else's discomfort? We pause in frustration at these impassable thresholds. Sartre, whose personal discomfort fructified into the virus of various absolutes during the last century, complained that you couldn't and made a career out of it. So many in imitation thus abstained and obtained temporary social status and perhaps sexual gratification by dittoing ad nauseam his distress at trendy parties in the sixties! How many babies were born thus! A generation, an entire generation! A generation stranded at the threshold of self-mirroring hatred and disgust on account of the musings of an insidious madman, a stained-birth malcontent, condemning life ad nauseam to the status of a stomach growl. May you rot in hell, you self-righteous prick!*

☿

I am writing about Layson because she has presently invaded me, or rather her presence infused me, interrupting the text supposedly addressed to Thea I had been forging, her virally infused erotic presence that is, but to say erotic is to condemn myself before you and many others who might read this, I would much rather find a haze of imprecision, of imprecise definitions, to spray over the perception of the horizon of her presence, that remains in me and has presently pervaded me, retains me, this smog preventing me from perception, from perceiving her presence, and I don't know whether it is really her presence, her present presence, where she is now, or the imprint left by her presence on me, her virally infused presence, or simply the perception of her acts acts as a virus on me, or my memory of my perception of her acts, infused, gestated, reached maturity, finally, seven years later, no more an imprint but a full performance, her present presence, I am spitting forth a plethora of inspired non-definitions aspiring to spit paint a spray of definitional imprecisions—"the sense of meaning is a trying to say," as my poet said—but I must pause here to consider number seven

⚲

It has been said, and I am inclined to believe it, though I don't know why, perhaps because the number seven has always carried for me an entrancing though unquestioned mystery—being content merely to carry it along, along with a few other personal adornments of immaterial essence, of the essence of thought and desire—that you are an entirely different person than the one you were seven years ago, on account perhaps of the fact that it is supposed that your cells, the entirety of them, are replaced with the passing of each seven years. If I were to pause to try conceive how someone, using whatever scientific instruments—I know nothing about science— were to calculate the changing of the cells, what I am saying is that even now, as I strain to imagine this process of calculation, all I come up with is the straining. We who have no access to scientific knowledge which is got via scientific experiments, we who are forced to get our knowledge second hand, and yet we accept it and in conversation repeat it to others, in houses, in apartments, at various gatherings, on the streets, in cars, in restaurants, sitting or standing, lying down near our longed for, in order to facilitate the passing of time in a more constructive manner. Yes, we are merely grateful to receive a morsel of knowledge, which we can use to pass our timeframes in a more constructive manner. Our predefined timeframes pleasantly. Thus the time passes constructively and then, it's the end. This information we repeat much less, though we have direct knowledge of it. Second hand too but direct. They just don't come back. We mostly repeat it, not the one about the end, in order to assure ourselves that, in order to assure ourselves, and when we do, we are standing or we are sitting, rarely when walking, but when walking we're not walking very far, we're walking merely soon to be sitting. Our movements are so minuscule. I have thought that perhaps this information, this sort of knowledge is spread among the populace by people while sitting or standing, in other words, while our movements are minuscule. Perhaps this information is spread among the populace to insure that its movements, the populace's, are minuscule and thus prevent larger movements which might lead to social unrest and even political upturn. Thus what is achieved through the spreading of this knowledge is the minuscule movements of each of the members of the populace, which, in order to make the time 'more easily passing' is forced, by the fact of his or her being fed this, and other, knowledge of this sort, in other words knowledge which is got through scientific experiment but which may not be verified by the receivers on account of the fact that, first, they have no access to it other than the mouths of those from whom they hear it, and then they are so grateful to have received it they mostly pass it on for the reasons described above, second, even if they should wish to verify it in their troubling inner moments, even if they should wish to do so and within themselves and protest bitterly, within themselves, at their lack of ability to verify this knowledge at first hand, knowledge which their inner sensors, inner sensors which they have long given up on, or been made to give up on, tells them to verify. But, how could they verify it? They have not spent their time wisely while in college—who has?—and thus scientific knowledge is prevented from reaching them, or they are prevented from reaching it. They are now forced to enter the work-force, they are slaves in service to the weekly social masquerade. They are slaves in service to the passing of weeks. They are slaves in service to the factory of fashioning of the common desires. Their desires, brains, arms, legs, their minuscule gesticulations, all in service of the procreation of more desire leading to more production. What's the difference between people anyway? There are those whose lives are involved in making production, there are those whose lives are involved in making desires for what is produced. None much of what is produced is of much value. The only hope left is that their cells may completely renew themselves within seven years and this gives reason for hope. Who has time to investigate a hunch? When I say hunch, I mean the information which is provided them by their inner sensors. Certainly there are those whose inner sensors may at moments be more powerful than their inner censors. Protest bitterly against their inner censors. But who has time for them? Still, the inner sensors of some, even in their atrophied form, cause them discomfort. Thus, a third, tributary group: those in charge of stilling the inner sensors. Still, as the inner sensors do not still easily, atrophied as they may be, those in charge of stilling them must invent more efficient manners of stilling them. Thus those in charge of disordering terminations such as depressive disorders, social anxieties, panic disorders, obsessive compulsions, compulsive obsessions, twitching, tremor, mania. Poetry too can be made to be used in service of servitude. Thus more production, in service of production, because one in the grips of his or her troubling inner sensors which will refuse to be censored, may not proficiently be employed in service of production. More production, I mean, of stupefiers, of stillers, of the production of the inner sensors, which have been long atrophied by disregard as their production does not in any way conform to the needs of the current modes of production. Merely to maintain the present modes of production, we are producing stupefiers to censor and still the sensors that still insist on protesting their stilling. They must be trying to tell us something, though because we have so long stilled them, we can't discern what, nor do we have the energy to listen, let alone proceed along the routes they warn us. Yes, they are still there, unstilled, insisting, because present modes of production are engaged in the production of vast amounts of stupefiers to still the result of the unstilled and still insisting inner sensors.

☿

Layson, you stepped out of the orders of Morpheus, disordering consort to the daily quotidian, commando of whirlwind and quicksand, sister of Hysteria, the green whip of dreams, chimerical kidnapper from the orders of longing, beholden-to-none cavalier of disappearance, warden of swords and troubadours, in your nights you take off my days, I am now a willing and combusting number in your nights, a lost soldier of petroleum and verdigris, a spider-web unfolding in reverse as my nights become your days, your days patrolling my nights, my days secretly marching inside the secret of your nights, inside the nights of your secret...Layson, your reflection now turns blind stone to mirror.

Where are the towers, the fountains, the plazas, the balconies you proclaimed? The plans for vertigo you espoused? It is to tame this contamination of quicksands that I write. Oh spider! Was it only air you wished to make?

☿

But I need to come back and speak of what I began to speak of earlier, "imprint on me", and when I say on me I am being inexact to be sure, perhaps to be inexact is the purpose here, my purpose, I

29

confess I thrive on, splurge in inexactness like an enrapturing vice to delve in, I could say, in place of me, on my soul, I could actually venture, at least in print, to say my soul, to say soul, it would be a veritable act of daring to put soul in my own text, to concatenate the massy convolutions of my personal feverishness with the soul, that would indeed be an act of daring, an act of veritable and admirable, I would dare say, audacity, a challenge to forces which you rarely consider, you rarely stop to consider as involved in your personal feverishness as you go about the world involved in, you say the soul, and perhaps, in order to feel safe you might wish to say the Soul, how can you even mention in the text the vice above mentioned so close to the soul, originally a few lines up the word soul came up merely as a figure of speech, without any awakened consciousness of its vast implications. I spoke about being inexact, of my complacent indulgence in inexactness, but this is not what I mean, you can't merely resort to this word out of hand, like simply resorting unconsciously to a figure of speech when speaking while those half-listening to you and waiting for the punch-line are missing the vaster implications of your figures of speech, they go about their world without further pausing to consider the implications of any figures of speech, these lives go on without any awakenings, in these people's parts, these people who play their part to feed you sometimes, sometimes to sleep with you, sometimes to hire you and pay you, never stopping to consider the vaster significances of figures of speech and language snakes alive below their unconscious meanderings through their circumscribed and circumscribing mundo, their lives no more than floccinating about, as I said in my letter to Thea:

... so, don't rush to the end or skip through the text thinking that if you get to the end the big mystery will be solved, resolved or revealed and your curiosity will be satisfied. Take your time reading it. Each word counts. I know that you are impatient by nature, trained as you are by the forces of the industrial revolution and utility, forces inimical

to poetry, take a big breath, settle in the armchair in the living room, if your music stand is not presently standing on it, and read slowly. And look up every word you don't know, don't just jump ahead. Get the nuance. That has always been your major failing, you flunked nuance. No, more, you abused nuance, nuance always made you unsteady and gave you irrational spills. I know you will hate me for this. I can see your sudden fingers twisting like living roots that plunge into the pages of this letter and my beautiful words are now no more than the crumpled paper which you now trample on the floor. All my beautiful literature destroyed! But I know you! You'll crumple on the bed, you'll sleep fitfully, protest against the cruelty of the impending day, then glue the paper patiently back together, (the tape is in its place on your table, neatly in the holder you stole) I bow to your uncanny patience, the precision instilled in you by the centuries of your superior history. There are, admittedly, advantages to growing up in the kneading fingers of colonialist nations preparing its young for imagined future conquests from whose still-trickling profits we still imbibe. Still, you are one of those who in the poetic future (which my words will bring about along with the downfall of the present) is to be admonished before the law, if not tried for making nuance unpopular and don't imagine I will be there once again to speak impressively on your behalf. She was inimical, I will tell them—and thus denounce you—to my aroma of ineffability. On the other hand my aroma of ineffability made you delirious and you slashed at the flesh that bore it, though careful at times not to break it. Your intolerance with my fetish for the infinitesimal is notorious, as well as my fetish for endless recapitulation. But despite my lack of present notoriety—how I unhinged you when I perfidiously tore up the present as I pleased without any fear of the future—I have always been a challenge to the present's enthusiasms. But for now, steady yourself. It may be, like I said, you may never ever hear from me again. I mean never in this lifetime. Perhaps in the next, but that's a long time and then you've got to go through childhood all over again. I repeat, this may be our very last communication. I have a reason for saying this repeatedly, I am not merely "blackening the pages with words". As I said, you must destroy this letter, despite the time you spent gluing back together, as soon as you have finished reading it. If you think this is bad news for you, imagine how I feel, because I recognize there is some excellent writing in parts, and I can't resist wishing to publish it. I can't resist wishing it were a book. You will not be able to go back to it once you've skipped through it. Think of the time you read it as time spent together with me, the very last time spent together with me. Make each word count. Say it out loud perhaps. Say it clearly and enjoy its passage through your throat, your palate, your teeth, its tangy shape on the tongue, this spicy Saussure sauce, how it shapes the circulation of your blood, your vascular system, the surrounding space. Words are life. Words may be short, but only if you picture life as being long and the words as separate entities, entities separate from life, in other words, you may feel that, though being found inside life, as objects, say, are found under glass in a showcase, words do not share the same substance with life. It's like as if you pictured life as a general sort of greenish passage of time under whose post-gloaming deep purple vault over the tree tops streaked with furrows of clouds tinged with wisps of crimson and orange you were forced to endure this passage, and words as one of the things that you found under this vault, like fish in an aquarium. The glass and the fish are separate substances, arbitrarily forced to share space, but in essence have nothing in common with each other. They are not of the same material. It's like saying "a green monologue". I have never seen people pause under the purple to consider that life is words. Because if for instance green is a word and not necessarily merely the color of Rilke's laurel with its "tender ridges at the rim" and monologue is a word as well and not merely the uninterrupted sequence of words of a single person on a rostrum, then green and monologue are bound by the mere fact they have their glottality and their wind-expelling in common. Green monologue. Stop and say it. Do not go on with this till you stop to say it. Have you said it? Still to say green monologue, it is on account *of what each signifies which clashes in their concatenation and causes you vertigo, while the fact they are both words forms a federation. As for me, as I said before, I shiver to see myself rush to rub the skin of my pulsating heart against it, this green monologue, if merely for the duration of a distended diastole, my demurring tongue aspiring for the hurtling pause of a diphthong, this green monologue suspended on the high wire of my vocal chords, my hands of high wind. But you, in your utilitarian pursuits, forged by the march of molarity and more, you are entirely unmindful of, you pay no attention to the fact that even your blood is made up of words, vibrating, pullulating words, words like a steam of tiny quivering worms issuing from a Baudelaire cadaver, words uttered by beings we'll never meet, beings we've never met, our intestines too are words, our livers are words, our eggs are words, our hands are words, our fingers are words, our toes are words, our genitals are words. Your genitals are words. Your breasts are words. Your breath is words. I will go on with this list, which I may never complete, because it is endless, incessant, but please don't skip through it, simply assuming I am listing body parts selected in an arbitrary manner, body parts you are familiar with, don't assume you 'know' what I am talking about and take this list for granted. You know how I hate lists. It is essential that you do not skip through, I must insist you take up no uncertain arms against your tendency to skip through this passage giving in to the utilitarian tendency and assume it is repetitive, as for instance, the word words, which repeats itself each time, so you would just not read it again. I know you, you wouldn't. I can see you now, not doing it. I can see you now stubbornly turning against it and skipping. Just curling up in the chair, stubbornly insisting on early sleep while murmuring Mozart under your breath. But it is essential that you read it each time so when I say your eyes are words, your teeth are words, your tongue is words, your navel is words, your pubis is words, your skeleton is words, your black stockings we bought with uncertainty at Pictoria's Intrigues, this is not a catalogue merely to fill up your time. Unsparing your glottality in service of one word, one word after another, the same* word. *The same word followed by another and then back to the same word. And so on. While the kingdoms of ennui bare their fangs from below, melt the coagulations of sub-obscurity. Dissolve the coagulated eventualities. No I am not merely making a catalogue to fill up your time. These are things you must know. These words dancing before you across the blank of the paper never to be intimated with lips, never to pass into ears, into stars. Am I reducing it all to the mere flatness of words across the alabaster? As though there were no such things as the petroleum of enraptured shivers and decomposition, stabbings and smokestacks, the horror of equestrian intrusions, orgasmic worms contemptuous of proper flesh. Indifferent to my frequent plunges into transcendence that your oceans of murmurs have afforded me. Oceans of murmurs the refuse of worms. So many generations on their resume. Imagine. If they kept a resume. Oceans of murmurs make the world go round. Imagine oceans of murmurs writing resumes. Oceans of murmurs reading books. They could read at night without a lamp because they coruscate, coruscating in capitulations of wet defeat.*

So you must each time read the word words without rushing, you must train yourself to do so, lend, more, abandon yourself to the process, force yourself even, yes force yourself, just as you would when you play your viola de gamba, you play each note fully as you hold it tight between your thighs, allowing it to reverberate fully, you play each note of each passage even when they repeat themselves. You don't skip through a passage because the notes repeat themselves. You don't say I already played that note. You do not protest against the repetition. But you confuse words and their significances, you opt for significances while disrespecting the words, you rush to grasp the significances and step on the words, and in so doing you do them a disservice, you disrespect them like a man who ignores the woman to get to the sexual act; you must unearth this perverse tendency you have and become cognizant of it and its roots in teutonic utility; its roots in the industrial revolution, when, in order to force it to occur, they were forced to force significances upon the poor words, whether they liked it or not, without taking the time to ask them; no, you must ask the word for permission to use it. More, they are in charge. Either they allow you to use them and then they spread across the page as they see fit or you're forced to write a report. You must return to this source and unearth this perverse prostitution of words; because unless you do so, you will always be a slave to utility, which is the purpose inimical to your purpose, you are defined according to the rules of utility whose purpose is not your purpose; thus you place your satisfaction in assuming you understood, or dissatisfaction in assuming you misunderstood, (which is more often the case with you,) before the reading itself, you wish to get away, make off somewhere else, with your understanding of what the significance of the text is, for no other purpose than to satisfy another and not yourself, secure in your somewhere else retreat and satisfied with your understanding, an imagined societal rostrum where you are not invited unless you show up with this misconstrued and severely severed understanding, or frustrated on account of the fact that the text doesn't lend itself to your misconstrued understanding, and if you do understand it you assume you have understood and in so doing you flagrantly ignore the purpose of the writer, who wrote the word words numerous times for a purpose. In ignoring the writer's purpose you are in fact not only being ill-mannered and discourteous to the writer but missing the writer's purpose, assuming that you understand it because you see a word, in this case words, that you understand, a word whose significance you easily grasp, a word whose significance you assume you have easily grasped, an easy word you do not have to bother to make the effort to look up, you do not have to contort your cortex to receive its true and various messages, you do not receive the word as a messenger of history or of the future, as an envoy and herald of innumerable beings, witness to unspoken and concealed facts and acts throughout time, history even, witness to an unrecorded secret history, greet it, rather her or him, from afar, with respect and joy, bow to them as you would to a being of "great courtesy and felicity", pronounce them with feverish gusto, with fervor and delight, place them on an altar of light. It is as though within their circumscription awaits a revelation so vast and so unexpected, as though the borders themselves whose duty is to circumscribe, to define a territorial intransigence, are mystic agents to transport us to a realm of infinite possibilities, as though a fo(u)rth dimension opens, this despite all arguments invented against them. But you, you merely want to know "what happened"; you do not even have to walk over to where the dictionary is (because I have never seen you, despite your training in teutonic precision and penchant for preparation, I have never once seen you take the precaution to place the tenth edition of my crimson hardback Merriam Webster's Collegiate beside you when you read), and because you have put your life in the service of utility, you simply assume you can skip through the passage rather than allowing yourself to follow the passage reading each word in the time that it takes to read each word. Slower even. Elongating the saying of each word as you salivate over it. As they say, chew slowly. Swallow slowly. I despise you for never pausing to demur, like a presentiment of roses throttled by neglect, demurring to measure them as fate rather than symbol. Demurring by no more than a mere mora, o that plunge of the unrepeatable hurtle! And you, you who opt for meaning! Meaning: ghouls rising from the clay, attempting to define it. It is the clay should be defining ghouls, clay out to define its ghouls, could never imagine it, do not even try. Yet clay and ghoul are unseparated, could you imagine the who and the what seeking a divorce? The ghoul emerging on its own, an independent puff. Do not put rouge and powder on this term, except by the power of this puff. Do not discard the diphthong, but do not distend the diastole! Yet you begin to protest now because there is already turbulence in your brain, you are beginning to become agitated and a surge of fury is beginning to eat away, to tear at the tenuous rope holding back the fist-waving crowd. They must be fists of sweaty common men, tillers of the earth, derrickers of petroleum, diggers of mines, transmuted by the ages into the beer drinkers of the filthy metropolis, the hungry crowd, the bare barrel-chested miners of the metropolis, O'Hara's silver hatted, Neruda's workers who would rather watch you naked on TV, protesting against being trapped inside the oneiric labyrinths of my good words, the toiling masses flailing against these word admixtures, which bounce off their cortex like billiard balls. Terror apprehends them as the word police surrounds them, swinging at them the batons of multiple inconclusive interpretations. Let them misinterpret the intricate black lace of your panties and then give them a beer, they'll be happy then, then let them out. Take a deep breath, close your eyes and imagine the blood of the sun coursing through your veins, your cells. "Bathe in the sun's waterfall." Everything comes from the sun, even lace and petroleum. Even the dun labyrinths. Go back to the text now, abandon yourself to the process. Abandon any desire for understanding according to the dictates of the police of utility. "Let the sun come bursting through your forehead."

Suddenly toads pierce the air
Entombed in a mystery of snow

☿

Words are free. Words are quivering electric worm-quantums forming what you are, decomposing compositions, whose significances are uttered by beings whose erotic phantasies we are. We are nothing but words which in essence are the erotic phantasies of beings whose significances we are and it is not our purpose to comprehend those significances, we must merely love them, be entranced by them, enraptured of them, even entrapped by them, worship them, be them, live them, and merely to attempt to comprehend the significances as abstracted extrications from the words themselves is to transmute the enjoyment to a personal inferno, to a terrifying desiccated suffering, a constricted, castricated, inward turning desiccation, sort of a paralysis where the fingers of your hands, of their own accord, like the tortuous twisting of the branches of the crepe myrtle in winter in the American south, turn inwards like a skill-less stage actor's attempting to display distress. I speak thus as a herald and envoy of these beings I speak of. Caveat comprehender! While the desire to understand is understandable, there is no need for it. To rush to the conquest of an anxious understanding, to teach the imprecise in marble hues, to assist the passage of an historical error, ah, the greatest of errors! I myself don't understand! I don't understand what I write. I don't understand most of what I read. I don't even understand much of what I translate. This will come as shock to you, but rather than meaning I look for the mold in words. It's soft and warm like a verdigris longing, like a mother of intangible milk. I feel them for leaks, particularly underneath, it's a special skill I have developed, hunter of hunter-green moss, the verdigris grind, is entrancing to the tap of the tip of my fingerprints along the hyperboloid belly. I grow with putrefaction and fungus. I invade space with my big smile and my inner light and my aura, I deceive them all, I invade with my empire of putrefaction and fungus, with its hanging mist of ultimate betrayal, with its faltering language of ultimate betrayal, and how you adored that language and how it made you wait by the gate, the iron gate for so long, before you got in when least expected

I invade with putrefaction and fungus,
an emerald fluctuating tongue permeating the mist
A dubious penetration of rust and Magdalene shifting Magdalene
Osiris with a trombone across the seam of insubstance,
a seam uneven to the climb, Hymalayas, empires, quiverings
whose fascinations are the motive schemes of the day.

☿

The meaning mostly belongs to them who are goaded by urges whose sources I suspect. I am not from around here, I don't belong to this race, as the poet said. They may have infected the words with meanings whose range poisons the race. The meanings reach the tips of my nimble thin fingers, seeking comfort and sex. It is my job to disinfect them. This is my job. How I do it is my own business but most of the choleric syndrome in my aspect that I've caught and you've commented on is professional hazard, if you get what I mean. I am afraid that I am more than stained, I fear I am tarred. I scrape it off daily, furiously for no glory, no future glory I can discern, but it persists. Where is the glow I crave? I tried alchemically boiling it in a mistaken nebula; the ingredients were imprecise, the expected result unforthcoming. (Why are you so imprecise, the adjudicator inquired amidst the gun-toting yard animals. He had recently stepped in, having just studied his eidolon in cinematographical penumbra.) Now I live only for the future because I sustain with a sigh the faltering faith in the memory that my fault is not congenital. I do not know how others maintain faith. A congenital rock of rubber. Faltering oscillates like thin steel foils when provoked. Do not burden yourself with understanding. It is here that a bouquet of genuine indifferences makes all the difference. Cultivate that. But, how cultivate that! I know you will ask it. There are gardens where they are taught, under the purple, under the breathy sway of the green selenic fronds where impalpable beings inspire from unsuspected hymns. That is to be suspected. Suspected. Not yet found. Perhaps to peer at will incessantly under the breathy sway of the green selenic fronds. By gurus of indifference. Indifference has become a costly commodity around here and only those few who mastered it might hold the banner to the footfall of progress. The rest of us tremble and shake obsessively in incursions of self-organized oppression.

☿

Oh my Thea, how long have I spent attempting to strip the words of their meaning! How I mixed them up meaningfully. How they became proclamations of nothing. But you could take nothing and drop it on the table and it would jingle like gold coins!

☿

Do I wish, you may ask, to become the Queen of the Underground? Somewhere below New York City, between the subway and the chase, the impending rap of the wheels and desire, the zither in a hurry, leaking a deadly hatred and evolution, dismissing all in my diseased corruption, I discharge a hazardous state, a child of abductions, lexicides that place the populace at greater risks than any contamination.

☿

The Grand Sorbet of Tamara was plounging in the Mood. He was extricating Savants from their lovely Manulet. He twirled it so once or several and grids collided on their way to the coliseum.

☿

AN INTERLUDE

a few scattered fragments torn from a discourse
on words and meaning

the unit of understanding, the word, containing the cognition that surrounds it, the cognition that emanates from it, like the light of a sun, and the world it claims and carves for itself in the mental field, the territory it appropriates, the constant shifting, swirling of meanings shifting the sense of awareness in the mind; the fluid fence guarding a concept from other concepts, guarding the concept's meaning from other meanings; thus concepts too can be nationalistic and try to protect their own meanings from the invasive incursions of other meanings, invasive meanings hoarding new meanings on board, captured or willing, nomad meanings in search of acquiring new homes of meanings which did not belong to them or which they did not belong to or which, perhaps, wild in their incipience, undomesticated, had pruned the shifting motions of meanings, of secondary and tertiary meanings, of hues of meanings which have obscured the original stationary meaning around which the nation of meaning was formed, the nomad meanings being nothing but a call from the core of the stabilized meaning of the nation, from the still wild heart of the pruned meaning to its wandering, roaming brother for help to return to its undomesticated origin meanings attached with tar to the word, the word sullied by meanings through unpleasant associations—thus the expression 'the tar of unpleasant associations'—this harks back to the nationalism of the word/meaning/cognition unit, though, again, we cannot call it a

but the word is not a station from which to attach meanings, with tar or what have you; the word and the meanings and the simultaneous cognition are one; a silk wrap of meaning threshold surrounds the word-meanings; the meanings, like a pajama party, thrash inside the silky threshold, searching to expand and escape into new meanings, make new friends, combine and shift meanings by thus combining; though we won't admit it, it loves to combine with languages the conscious effort regards, judges as 'foreign'. This expansion is not political, or colonialistic: it is simply life in search of erotic expansion; a yearning towards transcendence of all barriers, alchemy of the word

associations: the primary word has associations—it is only through the associations that it can claim any identity—some of whom are trustworthy and loyal, loyal hues, while others are trystworthy, inclined to 'making new friends' (hues constantly chattering away, unwary and uncaring of the imminent danger of dissolution they are constantly in) these new friends whose intents are either surreptitiously inimical to the primary word, intending to capture it for purposes of new meanings, its own purposes of expansive meanings (or even other, unknown purposes whose perfumes are vague, ungraspable, or perhaps grasped only by the very skilled and even then with difficulty), or plain whimsical, associations that are not of long term interest, thus freely intersecting and forming short-term friendships which nonetheless lead to the dilution of the meaning of the primary word in the peripheries, which returns by-and-by to the origin, through the associations, which have no power to hold on to their original meaning which only had staying power in relation to the primary word but which was too limiting (they felt); the primary word, can be said, was only concerned with maintaining the personal power of its identity and was using the weaker hues to reflect its power in; and the weaker hues, in need of a primary word to reflect but not having identity of their own, shimmering hues on the perfumed sea, are open to, sensitive to, other secondary meanings, to which, poetic souls that they are— Verlaine made them so, gave them that sort of identity—are happy to ally themselves to these brief or longer term affairs, some of which reduce them to nothingness, some of which enrich their meaning to where hue becomes primary color and the primary color loses its fame and falls into disrepute (or disreputed hue, dysfunctional hue, out-of-fashion hue). Other times these meanings attached to them become stained with a vicious tar of various other meanings, which is nearly impossible to scrape off. And the brain, like a fly helplessly attempting to scrape off the glue it has landed in with its free legs but only spreads it wider over the rest of its body, thus imprisoning itself all the more, such is the fate of words in a brain that can't remove undesired meaning from its own word clusters, much as it wants to, which is entrenched in the meaning of its words, like a fly in glue

the particular: the hospitable mind that welcomes the particular floating up to the fore of the mental field one fine day on the bubbles of cognitive awareness and makes an example out of it. Shouldn't the particular, now as an example, thus no longer a particular, revolt against being made an example of? Is it too late to attempt a return back to its particular state? (Here we have perhaps the paradigm —erected out of a particular—of western culture's colonizing mentality), with innocent trust it floats to the surface like the friendly dolphin, unmindful of the mind's utilitarian, in the service of—will the particular now 'get wise' and refuse to return? The artist too, only too happy to welcome these dolphins as material for his purposes—holding up his stunning particulars—thus stunting them—as examples before the stunned crew—

Unexampled and probably never to be repeated

Providing we can find it

Would we hurry after it before it melts and loses its consistency among the traffic of ferrying to-and-fro thoughts? Could we, were we challenged to do so or even challenged ourselves to the task, be capable of keeping up with its mysterious trackings?

and in foraging into this matter via scientific means, such as we are, should one include examples drawn from the sense of one's particular paranoia? Should you hold up a particular, for example, as example to the fore, would it cry and scream like a newborn while you, the holder, you, holding this particular up to the fore before the stunned crew— stunned by the beauty of the particular you're holding up—you and the crew unaware, uncognitive of the severe distress you're causing the particular who didn't wish to be presented at the fore as example before the assembly, it only revealed itself to you so that you'd appreciate its beauty for yourself alone, it was a gift from the mysteries, or perhaps it was no gift at all, just a careless particular on a whimsical stroll, one to carelessly wander too far away from the core, unmindful of the danger of being captured by a ruthless artist out hunting for particulars, and held up as an example, no longer itself now, no longer a particular now but an example, to stand in for all particulars of that sort, or rather to be held up as an example for all particulars of that sort, held up in the most unpleasant way before the leering and gesticulating crew and you, also leering, facing the crew and holding it up this particular example as a dangling particular, as a forced example, a stunning particular in fuchsia or cobalt or emerald forced to be an example at the fore before, like a kitten held up by the scruff of the neck, a concert of barking dogs, and you all the while thinking you got something good there, something good to show the crew, the admiring crew

one's fear of persecution? persecution by the very events which are his spiritual bread and butter, so to speak, as he is, in his privacy, obsessed with these non-existent events? But the kitten of particulars is real!

non-existent? Ha! How could they be non-existent when they are a constant companion? When they populate one's brain, when they pullulate there like cats and rabbits? How could they be non-existent when you spend your time incessantly in the company of these events?

as for spending time in the company of these events, joyful time, playful, but does one's mother allow it? Why this feeling of wasting one's time, if not from the mother scolding one for wallowing one's time splashing like a kitten in the soup of these joyful events, always though, at the back one's mind the stern worrigrind of momvoice, the grindstone of mom's worrivoice. Thus, the mother in service of the State, an unpaid civil worker, engaged by the forces of Utility. The mother as a primary conductor for the industrial revolution. The mother who gives birth as a primary engine driving humanity to the state of technological robots; thus the mother, the seat of emotions, the destroyer of emotions they are never one-dimensional, but the dimensions pile up pell-mell in one's awareness; a hodge-podge of dimensions, in psychic space, like mad scrawls but not without harmony, choosing their own v(o)ices at will; does academic training help to arrange the dimensions in one's awareness in neat cubicles? Like paying one's bills on time?

the routines of conceptual elements are drills in the service of the absolute whose purposes, alas, are to us a mystery. Armadas of word meanings charged with the power to cause us drills we goose step to despite our intimate fixations whose cages we visit by poetic word abduction, whose catacombs we tumble into whenever a poet's word is hiding around the unexpected corner of a concept whose meaning we fixed and formed a forced army around to protect, bands of words in intimate apparel feeding on our roots

"thoughts do not need powder and rouge," a drunken Tibetan mystic said. Not unless they're going to a party, of course. And they're always going to a party. So much for Tibetan mystics

the routine, after the 'route', the traveled way, the beaten road, where all travelers report the similar experience. Yet, the second traveler, wishing to please the first, enraptured perhaps by his personality and enthusiasm, dilutes his report with slight distortions to please the first and dittoes it; this becomes routine, "the way it should be." The third traveler's experience differs more than slightly, yet, hypnotized by the words of the first two, he aligns his experience with theirs, perhaps wishing to please, or become part of the club. All the while ignoring his intimate experience, longing, imagination, sexuality

for years I drilled the tendrils of my neurons in a goose-stepping concert till, at last, they became like a trained armada whose precise motions formed a micro-projector, an acoustic microscope, to pick up on her heart's desires, to play their reckless abandon back to her at an ever increasing velocity, until, like a vanquished Gulliver, like a Mozart sonata attempted on intestinal strings, I would abscond with their excessive stirrings to a precipitate of hypothetical moon I once spied in the emerald glimmer of her knees

he had honed an invisible performance on the microscope

till I abandoned myself to a persistently recurring tremor she was setting in motion by pursing her lips in imitation of her earthword armada she persistently trained in her daily nursery

should I abandon myself to a cognition not my own as barter for the mask of similes? For the welcoming embrace of statutes? I much rather should abandon myself to the embrace of a nest of cognitive worms, electric this playful particular left no paper trail

this pasquinade, straining to hoist up the words to the level of wit on the parbuckle of social consent

the epithelium dissolves like a sugary restraint, the currents sweetly suck you into meanings you've never dreamed of which nevertheless are slightly familiar like lovers whose intimate longings you've long ignored, out of malice, out of modesty you no longer suspected encumbered you, constraints remaining like an unpleasant remembrance painted over in the strident hues of compromise agreements: but you are now whirling in the whorl, you are inducted into pleasant forgiveness by meanings who love you and long for you, better yet, desire you without shame, without conditions, invite the same of you with wily smiles, stir you with disobedient similes, welcome you and dissolve you into their levels and like a spice adopt you as a long awaited opiate, a leader of dreaming sugary armadas...

armadas of negative scouts, bereft of meaning within but painted with the bright purpose to deflect by denial the pointed arrows loosened by the incessant archers of the intrusive new associations, whose black market contraband connections impinging upon the constraining concrete of mutual agreement meanings, leaping smugglers over the barbed wire surrounding the concentration camps of consensual understanding her porphyry pas de chat, the pas and the porphyry though inseparable events, yet the proud delicacy of the pas of the chat occluded, almost, by the explosive quavering, no less lovely, of porphyry; the shock of deliberating events, one of motion contra one of hue; it's as though sinking into slumber was called for here to absolve us of this dilemma. But in slumber, perhaps where she deliberately transported you with her porphyry ruse, where she could abscond with you on a mystery stage free of deliberation, there she had her way and you refused to deliberate, abandoned yourself to her catacombs of porphyry ruse, worshipper without consent

exponent of the particular being held up as example: in fact he is an exponent of the particular struggling against being held in derision as an example. Does the exponent care about the distress of the particular, the exponent when faced with the jeering critical crew, when being held up as example for criticism, it is this kind of particular behavior we object to, for example

likely to bubble up to the surface as hostile insurgent actions of the active imagination, particulars as time bombs, particulars like innocent dolphins which when held up to the applauding crowd as examples by colonizing artists who perform before the adoring crew

beg the forgiveness of the marine figures at the core, of the cephalopod fringes of the rusty central concepts at the core

There are no expressways for the words. But maybe there are. Perhaps at the level of words, the exchanges take place at much greater speed than we can imagine. Some word or another become functional to the quotidian masquerade, and thus worthy of being revolutionized; how does the revolution take place? How is the power removed from the false pedestal? How do we turn the pedestal into the cataphalque?

how do these exchanges take place? Are there some sort of messengers that travel from word to word, from cluster to cluster?

who has the right to expropriate a word of its meaning? Or rather expropriate the meaning from a word?

meaning of words as in current frame of usage, forced into meaning in the current frame of usage. Yet, just like the daily businessman who, as soon as he gets home, sheds the business suit for something more comfortable, so do words—as soon as they have spent the day in the straight jacket of meaning—head, at night, for the freedom of aphasia. Though some, like those who shed the suit for the negligee in the mirror, some words leave the straight-jacket of consensual meaning for the constraint of ritual meaning in the mirror. Though, as soon as they leave the mirror, if they are not imprisoned or killed, they spice up the consensual meaning and force it to change, not directly but through implication and seduction

in the realm of meaning, there are no meaning expropriators, I mean those expropriators whose express purpose is to bereave a word of meaning— why do I think of grieve?—there are movements of meanings whose purpose is beneath the surface to fathom, movements that lead to constant shifts of meaning, swaying like flowerbells at the bottom of the ocean, meanings in whose arms like Morpheus one sinks and dreams. Maybe I am the meaning shifter, maybe I shift meanings because it pleases me to do so; I will take your meaning away, and in its place I will fit a newer meaning for you to promenade in your straight-jacket the way you search your meaning in the meanings of others

or I will expurgate you of your grave meanings, bury them with cadavers at the bottom of the sea

causing the exsertile organ to distend whimsically, not for purposes of production

even if you forced a meaning upon a word who is not willing to encapsulate that meaning, the word would rebel.

The word is not a stone shape to which a meaning can be attached at no cost—all this above has to be rewritten to reach closer for the meaning a word is not a stone bowl into which the water of meaning can be poured. Because a word is not stone nor the meaning water

it is important to grasp the following: that words and meanings are a priori to people; they are cognitive entities as well; it just so happens that people and language come together in varying degrees. But the entity of language moves at its own pace and especially by its own purpose, regardless of people. People would do well to pay more attention to it; some are granted privileged views into its workings, are allowed journeys on its veining rivers; they should kneel and give thanks, those; it is a rare privilege. It is the privilege of him or her who is permitted to join life itself

I will bereave you of meaning like thin clothes and leave you to peer at yourself meaningless, without meaning in the mirror of the void but beautiful to my purposes

denotation is fraught with connotation; denotation dangerously shifts its mutational multitudes of meanings in the delusive waters of connotation; always the peril of drowning is present, the drown itself, fodder for the deeper fishes of meaning, the deeper fishes of dream, returns as newer, transmuted meanings, meanings with a past, meanings with a dolorous past, meanings encumbered by amnesia, meanings with stained or even recomposed identities, incomplete identities, vampirized identities, uncertain meanings, marginalized at first, but soon to recompose the armadas of mutual consents, soft guerrilla meanings, which subvert by seduction, the subversive seduction of the ignored and marginalized

not the liquid lapping of inquisitive *l*, neither the invasiveness of the primary *p*; yours is the insurgency of whispering, on the edge of shimmering sideways chimeras glimpsed in the spinning of a minuet of innuendoes

a word still in the formation of its meaning, still spinning new meanings, new connotations formed by the spin of its denotation on a stroll through the park where the fully and newly formed parade in their fineries, should not be wrenched from its formative spin to be placed in the march of the above mentioned parade; its obscurities will be apparent, its lack of yolk will make an unpleasant splash, its obscurities will discomfort like the sudden ghost on the tongue of the poet; still there will be those who retain that the unformed are perfectly formed to the open eye of the seer, and that the parade has grown entrenched in a concretized shape; that it has allowed the norms of utility to influence its whimsical realm; that it has succumbed to the stone, Greek concept of beauty rather than the pre-Greek African mystery as in the works on Amos Tutuola. There the seam between the formed and unformed is obscured and transworld travel is allowed, prominent and preferred

perhaps it is the craving of the unformed or not yet formed to exteriorize itself; such craving yet unboiled yet it will exterminate itself to be exterior

am I an extern to tongue? I wish to be an intern, tongue, let me in!

to be amidst language! an angel of language, absolutely free! A purveyor of words! A saltimbanco of the tongue. One trading in tongues. Word peddler! Contraband contrabad! Purveyor of tongue contraband intrinsic sussurates of the source, a source whisperer. One external to it is merely an exoskeleton

to lovingly re-invaginate the premature externals, premature externals which long for re-invagination. How long does it take for re-invagination to become reinvagination?

The difference between writhe and convolutions is a matter of time

do not wrench the meanings dreaming in-utero; to do so you prove to be circumscribed by a profound externalism; I must then wrench the meanings back from you and lovingly re-invaginate them, the premature externals

the extraction of this word is suspicious; but the words know each other well; they have traveled long roads together along the centuries which they do not know, their systems of calculation transcends ours and cannot be imagined or conceived by us with our present conceptual circumscriptions; it is only people who suffer because they do not attain to the level of words; to them words are immaterial and feed no flesh and blood; (though some feed on the limited mastery they have achieved of words), they live tangentially to the world of words, which they suspect, though they give it not much thought, that it is vast and unimaginable; they suppose someone goes there and brings back a few useful words, someone designated by the state or by the priests or by the lawyers. 'He is a man of a few words': what arrogance, what ignorance to admire such a man, what stupidity! As though the man himself owned those words! As though that man was given free reign over the word storage vaginas, to the pullulating crowds of words which are perpetually in motion and to which the affairs of men are beholden, though the arrogant ignorant men suspect nothing of it

but words wish to induce one to use who wishes to be their conductor; this one is inducted to carry their purpose; this is the word made flesh, rather, the words made flesh; compare to the power of the enemy whose primary weapon is television; the enemy, in order to function, to spread and broadcast its message, needs cash, money. The functionary of words needs only a dictionary and the will to fight; he is a virus carrier; he sets his viruses consciously and not; he is a messenger of the words whose function he carries; he infuses with his viruses unbeknownst to those he infuses; he is an Eulenspiegel, a whimsical sort whose purpose is to beguile, he is the poet-spy

the mind of the public made dull by television pays attention to the unformed, the ghostly, words, but not with the primary attention which has been captured by television; this is better, more effective, as thus the poet-spy can infiltrate in much more powerful and secret ways

the vagueness of the project and the convulsive effort with which one plunges into it

⚥

So here I was, about to say soul, Layson, and I don't know what soul is, I find myself protesting against my wishing to use it, this word soul, in this text merely as a figure of speech, a reducing and reducible trope merely for the sake of the text's convenience, or on the other hand as Whitman said, everything parts for the progress of souls, but Walt, we are here with Layson, tell me, hold me close, envelop me in the comfort of your white beard and tell me, hold me close Walt and tell me: what is it, the soul, I mean to consider it, it has been defined so imprecisely throughout history, either in literature or in theological texts and I know you know I couldn't possibly have read them all to settle for once, or for the provisional purposes of this text, on someone's definition of it, Saint Thomas of Aquinas' for instance, or Saint Theresa's, or Mother Theresa's even, or perhaps to settle on the official definition of it, Saint Augustine's perhaps, when in fact were I to force a representative of officialdom, someone with access to the magisterium, to present the official definition of the soul once and for all for the purposes of clarifying its electrifying but still ill-defined identity, the soul's, (and how we flail and floccinate in the attempt!), here I am attempting to clarify its identity, because the soul itself has not been very forthcoming in clarifying itself, making itself apparent, during the history of humankind, my personal knowledge of it in any case, from the books I studied or what I may have heard from friends in casual conversation or in lectures in the various schools I may have attended over the years, the soul seems, to my understanding, to my ability, limited as it may be, my understanding, that is, to ascertain, seems to have selected certain officials and official organizations to represent it, but I confess here, I declare rather, and rather audaciously, these officials have been poor representatives of it, and the soul has, to my knowledge, rarely come to the rescue, as though it—I don't know if it's appropriate to use 'it' for the soul, but it is the congenital fault of this language I have been forced into, forged into, forgotten into, and yes you may say I may use, say, "she" for it, She, but presently I don't wish to discriminate, it is not presently the right time to discriminate, not now, not yet—as though it didn't care, as though it weren't its concern, you can clearly discern here that my general view of it, of the soul, is a positive one—I say this not out of fear—I liken it to certain accounts of splendor I read about, accounts I may have been privileged by (or with) by predecessors or even moments of first knowledge— and who can speak of those without preaching—but still, one asks here and rightly so, I shouldn't put myself in peril if I simply asked, I merely wish to know, it couldn't do any harm, to investigate into the veracity, I doubt the orders of the soul—formless energies or Rilke-like developed beings, or even the legendary and maddeningly ungraspable blending fusions whose fulfilling you crave, those effusive fusions of *who* and *what*—I doubt they would object if I asked, to ask is not a sin, why the soul in general has chosen such poor representatives on earth? That is a mystery to me, is it perhaps possible to speculate here that perhaps the soul has not chosen them at all but these officials of the soul have merely claimed on public rostrums to be its representatives, its trumpeters, masters of pomp and tribunals, what if I said 'her' rather than 'its', brutal and fearful masters, so I wish to bring the correct definition of the soul, speak soul, speak, both for my benefit and for the benefit of all those between whose fingers these lines might fall, or whose eyes might fall upon these lines, whose patient eyes, patient like in hospitals, sanatoriums, patient in all its meanings and on the other hand, because certainly if I brought up the soul in the words that form these lines before you I must, must I, by all means bring up the correct definition of it according to standards, official standards, the magisterium, in order that I do not run the risk of being brought before the Tribunal of Official Definitions and tried with all due pomp before the tribunal for propagating it among the populace and infecting it with a view, a definition of the soul which does not conform to official standards—in case you're following the text attentively you might wonder why I switched to this sudden need to conform to standards, why I switched from the Mysterium to the Magisterium, I for whom standards are mere chewables for this expanded ad absurdum text, I am in case you're wondering, by no means recanting with its implications of History's plinths to Treachery and Betrayal—an inexact definition to be sure, I do not claim to be the bearer of the standard of exact definitions, this has always been far from my purposes as I see them, as I said, and perhaps a congenital deficiency at my core, fueled by self-, or outwardly imposed-, forgetfulness, but I do see its centrality, the soul's, its centrality is undeniable even to me and undisputed too, in our formulations of ourselves—I jump to first person plural here, if you caught it—adorning ourselves in its centrality, craving it like a fetish, we all agree upon its centrality in our formulations, our structures, certainly, we adorn ourselves with formulations of its structures, strictures, enforced group adorations, habit formations, professing procrastinations of prelapsarian delights (for what purpose?), proceeding from procrustean encrustments, the soul, crunchy, this abstracted venom invading our formulations, stepping along the paths of our venomed formulations, seeking the soul among the paths of our coagulated formulations, seeking its veritable venom to liberate us, speak soul

To return, Layson, or perhaps inexactness is what I demand, as much as, I mentioned it above, I wish to splurge, I long for it, like I long for you, for the imprint you left in me, reticulations rally, reticulations of imprints, or rather, to be exact in my splurge of indefinitions, I wish, I wish it, yes, I wish to splurge in inexact definitions, I myself crave to do this, revel in it, definitions opposed to the official definition, which must, by nature of the office of the official itself, be exact, but to return, I, an imprecise impresario of somnambulism, of languor and vertigo, a Siddhartha of fainting spells, I retain, now, seven years later, the afterwards of your presence like a convoluted mantle, a corruscant involucrum I can't peel off, a diamante striptease in reverse, a palpitation flecked with summoning, a sea calling out from inside an horizon of obscurity, an imponderable and convulsing remains neither physical alone nor simply spiritual, immaterial perhaps, but material, material because just like a material wrapping leaves its imprint on the skin, and a thin memory of it remains, so does this immaterial material leave its imprint upon the inner skin, I wanted to say the soul, what is this spiraling revolution within me merely by recalling her to mind, by using my powers of recall at will to recall her like a mnemonic device to incite demon-like the summoning, the call of this spiraling. As though I am being drowned in a vortex of soft promises, one that promises absolute fulfillment of ecstasy without end, or the pleasure of fulfillment without end, I don't know how to be exact here in pronouncing what I mean to say so I am mostly and to my shame as a writer floundering in approximations, floccinating, like my tongue, any tongue really, pronouncing sentence on myself as a writer, I am not succumbing to vulgate (but if I were, what?) but merely attempting to locate precisely the definition, as a tongue flounders about a clitoris in attempting to precisely locate it, do not discount what I say on account of clitoris and the act above alluded to, it is merely a scientific attempt at locating precision, using language, as first, flounder is an act of the linguist as he flounders about in order to locate imprecisely the precise location, definition, say it out loud, stop! STOP!

and say it: flounder, again, flounder, and observe, define the precise contortion of the tongue, then again, say it again, flounder, but this time peruse the shape the tongue assumes, not the tongue as it may be captured by the refraction of light on celluloid's silver, a limited device of reduced mentality—though not the silver itself, sister of the moon!—but the shape, like a contorted bird in flight, flounder's reverberation within you in consort with your tongue assumes when you have said it, mind you, this is not an instruction manual, or maybe it is, yes, it is, then further, peruse yourself precisely in the act, this is not for men alone, you know, this is for all, all should be poets and philosophers, I am being so extravagantly precise because it is so unbearably useless to be so, and I would wrap myself in it and parade in this precise wrap of uselessness in my neighborhood, shamelessly, solemn instigator of futile things (to paraphrase the man) strolling like a powder keg of fainting spells, simply to infuse a uselessness I assume they would never even appropriate as mode and manner, as formula, and yet hope it will be unleashed in their midst and all will succumb to it, and besides I find myself in need to be precise in communicating to you, my Thea, what I am feeling—if only someone had invented an instrument to measure the soul! To measure what I feel right now, when thinking of Layson, bathing in this memoiratorium—a healing of the soul, a fusion, rather a con-fusion with the alien universe, a completion of the being, a motion toward the complete fulfillment of the being. A birth, a death, a bath, a bathing. I am sorry to succumb to such quotidian nomenclature to define my journey about the Undefined. Who forces me to attempt to define anyway? Why can't life be a joyful splashing about in a vortex of the Undefined, a juggling of an array of imprecise definitions, after all isn't one an array of imprecise definitions anyway? Precise definitions are a rope to hang yourself with.

Sometimes, I venture to define, that Layson's imprint is, like that left by the memory, both enveloping and perused, of a clarinet. You will pause and be surprised when you see enveloping or perused in regards to a clarinet, if you paid attention precisely to what I wrote and not merely regarded it as pleasantly poetic fanfaronade. He's using clarinet as a metaphor, you might say, a trope, pausing briefly to scan a vague music within himself, yourself. A music you know nothing about, perhaps because you never take the time, from your utilitarian program, you never step down from your utilitarian scope, to investigate it. I am succumbing here to the temptation of a vague brushstroke of accusations, perhaps in order to circumvent an accusation leveled at my formulations, so confidently stated. I like formulations because the multiplicity of its significances reverberate so richly. And plicity in multiplicity signifies plication, plight, pliability, reverberates into an involucrum to delve deliriously into. Thus plight, and the deliriousness in its delicious hue. But before I detoured. I am summoned back by the clarinet. I am never not summoned back by the clarinet. It is as though within its circumscription awaits a revelation so vast and so unexpected, as though the borders themselves whose duty is to circumscribe, to define a territorial intransigence, are mystic agents to transport us to a realm of infinite possibilities, as though a fo(u)rth dimension opens, this despite all arguments invented against it. I am speaking in veils. I am taking the time to speak in veils. The clarinet too is a veil. I am speaking here to Thea, or to Layson, I am losing track who, veils have always been en(w)rapturing to my formulations, or perhaps I was thinking of someone who might be spying on me, reading this in order to be spying on me, it is not inconceivable nowadays, not at all, that even with the difficulties posed by this text, this veiled text, making it a daunting task, once you have entered, to maintain to the proper centripetal pathways, to avoid the suck of the centrifugal, not merely to maintain present orbit but to leap audaciously into ever closer ones, closer and closer to the suck of that imprecise center we crave, the sweet drops of liquid blackness, but still, someone might be found to trek easily through it, a poet might masquerade as a spy for the other side. Nowadays it could happen, do not be surprised by such betrayals. A spy could never masquerade as a poet. Only a poet might detect it. The surreption meant by the metaphor. What with the latest waves. This perhaps, I assume, or am afraid, in order to obtain the information to be catalogued, to be used against him. Or you. Me. (Because you might be seen as surreptitiously sewing in an immaterial weave of undetected terrorism.) After all, were we to rummage into the closet of the poet's personal metaphors, would we find that the metaphors were mainly a shining shield, the metaphor a glittering precious metal— immaterial material as it might be—to blind against the detection of a secret closet? Whose non-discovery might lead to undetected explosions to bring about the eventual end of the present? They constantly flounder in darkness about the present like it was a temple that might be constantly wrenched away from them. But to do so, you must constantly sink to deeper and deeper levels of surreption. In other words you embrace a surreption, a sweet surreption, I might add, you sink into a sweet surreption, simply to avoid detection. That is why I said before, not here, somewhere else, that the poet is a spy. Because in writing clarinet, I detected myself wishing to conceal. Though this is merely a letter to a personal friend, lover, it id, is, I mean, d is so close to s, likely to fall into the fingers of those who will use the information I was about to reveal but resorted instead to metaphor to distort me. I am palpitating, Thea, right now, merely to make the mere effort to imagine it, and the imagination itself is a clarinet, or the clarinet is imagination itself. Imagination is an inconceivable material, whose filigree I unravel, filament by filament. But if you say that it isn't, you merely prove your lack.

☿

It is not merely a matter of incarceration by shame that we must surpass, but the common denomination, the concatenation of precise denomination and precise gender, the praxis of precised gendering, meaning that the precision was not pre-exisent, but by-others-precised, so to speak, and formed or forced into common denomination, forced to serve, despite itself, denomination calling for public humiliation, denomination engaged by common consent to fabricate public humiliation, which is difficult to scrape off. (I have spied those perpetually incarcerated in personal scraping-off vendettas, all the while with a longing eye turned to the rostrums of re-denomination of precised societal gendering. Their plight is entrancing to me and at times, perpetually, like a circasia, I seek terrains to free them in.) I wish to add, this surreptitious disengendering, a terrain of catacombs not even the Song of Solomon sang, is a form of poiesis, unwritten yet perhaps, whose appreciative audience may be presently a denouncing spy. A re-denomination of the artist/audience affiliation. And it is dunked in surreption. I would say submerged in surreption, now after having said dunked submerged is far more entrancing to me, but the vulgar dunked summoned the guilty doughnut frosting bath I craved, not for long. But I admit it. Even if not for long, is it nothing if it is not for long? (It is nothing, I find myself moved to mention, to protest actually, protest is more correct, why crave I to be correct as I bathe, flail, in this dough batter against my better sense, no matter what I say I lie, it is nothing, I say, like the dough which is the imprint I spoke about above that Layson left upon me, the great wounding I had craved and the fountain that feeds this text before you.) And now I feel I need to scrape off the aftermath, the afterbath, with a vengeance, as these presently prevailing, these current and repugnant objects, among a multitude of current and repugnant objects presently prevailing and imposed upon the populace, of which I need incessantly to scrub myself, of whose concepts even I need incessantly to scrub myself, these objects and their implications do not belong in my writing, not even as concepts, unless of course transmuted and strained through the golden alchemical sieve in order to destroy their current distorted apparition, these objects whose present and abhorrent appearance in my writing stain it and I am tempted to select the last few lines and remove them completely by pushing delete. But who could promise me they would not prevail and stain me despite this apparently peremptory removal? Perhaps all the more so are we stained by peremptory removals. At least I am proceeding forward with the anticipation that continuing in the vein in which I had been, before the repugnant intrusion, departing from this vitiating port, will disperse their imprint completely in the next few sentences, but even to express this anticipation of dispersal, of this nauseating formulation, I had to pause and resort to a few moments' congress with the Region of the Unfathomable, or few moments of, at the very least, intoning at its gate. Or now, so tempting, to withdraw in your fur and your formulations, Layson, in the imaginal material of your fur and formulations, which is all I possess, my Layson, in which I wish to presently perish, to perish, yes, for no reason except that to presently perish in their presence is the greater life, or lie, I wish.

☿

This morning, my Layson, I delved into the book of their destruction and the cause of it—again I veil—and in it the primary apostle of their lord of destruction denominates himself—the denomination, I could discern, issuing from admixing his stained and ill mentality with ecstatic abandon—the prisoner of his lord, whereupon he proceeds to preach. As I myself, your apostle, I your prisoner, concealed in your fur and formulations, my Layson.

Make me well again. Make me a well, Layson, from which to spring a swill, an eruption to spurt forth the perishing venom upon their repugnant formulations, and, like a Gyno-Gulliver extinguishing the palace fires, forever to still them. Make me a seed and steed-like spurt me forth from your fur and formulations to spring again, anew the formulations I adore of which I don't yet know how speak. Make me that, Layson. Gush out my venom into a spring. And grant me the words to speak. Grant me the words to speak.

☿

You must return, in case you wish to ease the task of further reading—but pause awhile to ease the aftermath of previous spurting—to the first few sentences of the previous paragraph. I sentence you to return to those sentences. Perhaps, I myself do not remember, your sentence is to return two paragraphs back. It's a journey through personal time frames that I suspect will enhance you, as all sentences might. And then proceed to the next sentence. Or the one after the next. It is the it you must discern. I will defend it with definitions in these pages, pronouncing one sentence after the next, but can you defend it in public, can you define it precisely, so precisely as to forge a fashion? For if you forged a fashion and published it widely, against utility's suck, an enveloping fashion avalanching against the great utility, then men will step, one by one, two by two, en masse, away from their constricted course of reproduction's slaves. Yes to define it precisely, so precisely as to forge or force or fashion an avalanching fashion, but then, do you not hazard into the peril of being detected by those worthless object pushers, who will abduct your denominations for pushing their worthlessness unto the public to stimulate them to reproduction? The poet in service to the engineer? It's come to this.

It's come to this.

☿

I didn't mean clarinet. Like I said, I didn't mean clarinet, but I wished to hide something. I am not playing a guessing game, a guessing game with shame, I am not hovering about the border of concealing, or perhaps I am, but if you peruse closely clarinet and study it intricately, depending upon your lights, you will peruse what I meant.

But if you cling to conclusions you will die

☿

I felt entranced by hovering about the border of concealing, I wished to continue to hover around it, like a merry-go-round where you never reach the center, but you wish you could. Or know you should. And the wishing and the hovering—and not to say anything about the futility of knowing you should, because it is futile, sleep's suck has its way—opposing forces, make you sleepy, and you succumb to hovering as you sleep, but regretfully. The wish is to conceal and to reveal simultaneously, and you don't know which. It is a quandary that has you in its crepitating grips, like an iguana understood by suspicion alone, a quandary whose discovery turns you into a philosopher as opposed to one who merely wishes. Because you feel that concealing might save you, you don't know for sure, you think of revealing against concealing, you are at a stand-off that makes you sleepy, and longing. You can be neither a philosopher nor a mere wisher, or both, as though philosophy and wishing were at opposing poles. Or, you could claim, fearful perhaps it might be bragging, flashing poesy, while enrolled as a student at the academy of future night, you are safely sleepwalking barefoot on the edges of a soft zero. All this the entrancement of concealing, of revealing, the entrancement of this imponderable clarinet.

You were merely wishing a beating heart, unconcluded by anyone

☿

I wish to speak about it, I wish, as I mentioned, to be about it, what I meant to mention, I wished, wish, the enveloping plight, as well as the entrancement of perusal. In that manner this clarinet I speak of is complete, an integer, a whole containing both a within and a without.

The pause, the thin pause between here and there, *the* here rather, and *the* there, which is so short, this thin nothingness of a prohibition on which I madly tread to spite someone who is not. This thin nothingness and just as black and you are naked underneath. I might speak of course of its uses as an inducer of ecstasies. But I pause reluctantly, pause before the great reluctancy, though the enveloping and the perusal, concepts to be catalogued at opposing poles, are more than I can bear, and I wish to be about them, to hover about them in a self-conceived ad infinitum, but to my shame I am opposed and I pause before the great reluctancy. I must for the moment pause before the great demands of the great reluctancy and embrace instead sweet surreption. (And I am afraid as I continue that my language, by the demands placed on it, denses as I speak and so that it crumbles, like crumbling marl between my fingers.) I pause, prisoner of the great reluctancy, of which I am ashamed, before the task of which I spoke, before the task of re-denomination, of which I am presently ashamed. Before the task of de-concretizing the gendering. Still, it is from this hidden clarinet, pre-Layson fueled and re-fueled by her, that the present text springs, a weave I adore, I crave.

☿

I said, like the memory of a clarinet and I concealed. I didn't wish to conceal but I felt incarcerated by shame. But I must strip my own self-perception of definitions whose mirrorings present inclinations distorted by pre-conditioned popular jeer and rostrums of humiliation. I want to say what I wish to conceal. But if I say clarinet, if I nominate the concealing itself a clarinet, with its strands of coruscating notes flailing in the weave, or failing to protest against being woven, the coruscating notes but a feeble protest I adore, whose feeble adoring is in the fabric of all and even the core, if I summon it to be a clarinet and more, with its clear and complex implications, translucence and indulgence in forgetful weft

—but the indulgence itself has to be surreptitious in order for the vortextural abandon to occur—

if I summon the clarinet to be this concealing I am performing presently, and at great linguistic heights—a lexi-pyrotechnician who has honed his mania into superior technique—(this metaphoric modulation I indulge in!), this clarinet I speak of, clarinets, this must be specified, are such nothings that you will know nothing by the time you spend some time, *in scrupulous attendance*, in scrupulous attendance, softly sleepwalking on the edges of a soft zero, in a thin and tenuous dance, time with their names. You will know nothing, when you spend time in scrupulous attendance with the names I gave them, dance with the trials of my attempts to name them, "the watchful words that veil the enigmatic pleasure", as has been suggested: I am debating here for

> "momentous departures into being"
> each step a step into further
> imploding and imprecision
> and I am further debating
> I am summoning
> the speech of their vast speechlessness
> my tongue like a dictator fluent with channeling
> "denouncing the insufficiencies of reality"
> I, merely a harvester of steam

a ghost dancer among the carnivores
a serpentine & sinuous ghost throat,
amorphous with forms
"perpetually strolling through the heart
of the forbidden zone"
while a student at the academy of future night,
safely sleepwalking on the edges of a soft zero
I undulate among the voracious
nations and their history
Craving the plunge like a sweet malady
I too am a nation state
held in place by desire for nothing
that exists
that can be made
by a poetic wound,
inflicted in an ahistorical past plunged inside my clarinets
my failures in eternity
my fortress against their various absolutes
fortress against bathing
in the "density of commuters"
fortress against the habit formations
my clarinets
(quoting now from my Whitman who says he's not
too sure but is with me)
the unseen and the seen,
mysterious oceans where streams empty
prophetic spirits of materials shifting and
        flickering around me,
living beings, identities now doubtless near us in the
        air that we know not of,
contact daily and hourly that will not release me,
these selecting, these in hints demanded of me.
not them with a daily kiss onward from childhood
        kissing me,
have winded and twisted around me that which
        holds me to them,
any more than I am held to the heavens and all the
        spiritual world,
after what they have done to me, suggesting themes.

My clarinets:
You wrest melodies from what cannot be verified
with the result of roses
In you
I am committing obscure adultery in placenta
To obviate the anxiety of being impetrated
by congenital impetigo or pemphigus

☿

There is cohesiveness in clarinets I adore, like an entire people
adore their most recent saint. There used to be consistency in the
tenure of saints, which thinned out progressively with the progress of
these states, these blessed states, relatively blessed states, punctured
by tenure and oblique statements. But we must never adore their
mothering, infused with wrinkles and pogroms. It is only the marches
of the suffused genders we adore. In motion slowed to explain by
example, as necessary at times in the screenplays they flutter into the
disappearing horizon in weightless cream and rage. I too am invited
to disappear, I am now a disappearing act. To disappear into the wind
of disappearance, to be poetic, the metaphysical disappearance. To
live for years with shame next to the metaphysical disappearance,
and at night, without shame, with secret pride, to imbibe from it,
to peer

To wave my arms in the holes of nothing
To be ensconced in their reflux
Words that do not suspect me

☿

It is a major accomplishment to love poetry and hate the world
for so long

these clarinets whose entrancing existence is rooted in world wide trade, whose existence is a shining example for instance of world production, international labor, the excavation for petroleum in concocted coagulations whose dogmas cause you impenetrable and discomforting relationships to your seeking of the imaginal promises of the Erotic impulses, coagulations we war with, for your clarinets, a clarinet is then a tank, a suicide bomber, an air raid, a sortie, an escaped war prisoner, the enemy dead, our dead, the dead who no longer need them, who forfeit their own lives for the consistency of these clarinets, a multiplicity of meanings whose mass of apparently infinite world wide webs befuddle you should you attempt to decipher them, attempt to decipher them against the obstinacy of the Great Refusal, and the multiplicity of meanings that I am assigning to them springs from this fountain which is the imprint that Layson left on my being. I wanted to say left me dying with, but that may seem far too dramatic, yet in a literal way, true. I may be rushing to conclusions here, I may be eager, I see myself being eager, I arrest myself in my eagerness, to settle upon a reason, upon an easily secured island of meaning, I may be too eager to secure a patch of solid ground against the Great Refusal, against the workings of the Great Refusal, which may be my undoing if, if I cling to it too severely, securely, but what I see is a connection here because it is Layson who wounded me thus, perhaps from the very moment, the initial moment I spied her, in the Bodhi Tree Bookstore in Los Angeles, significant name, Bodhi Tree, the tree under which the Illumined One first achieved his Illumination by defeating Maya the Illusion, against the Great Refusal perhaps, wrenching perhaps his being out of the Great Forgetfulness,

But, first I want to speak about place. Because if it weren't, we would not have been and this would not have been. Remember where you are, so there's no confusion later. I mean remember where you are in this text, if you wish to follow it precisely in the manner of the meaning I mean. But as far as what you call physical place, and I do not speak of merely physical places with pleasure, it is not a pleasure for me to give you place, you may go there if you wish and see for yourself, that is your business, leave me out of it, it was in a bookstore named The Bodhi Tree, and it may be assumed that each person who came in to buy or to browse was a good person, a worthy person, someone to be trusted—this is what the books tell us— because, though they were not enlightened yet, otherwise why there? were in the bookstore because they wanted to be enlightened. Because every book in every nook and every cranny in that store was a book that was written in order to repair a wrong or to fix a fixation that vexed human beings, these human beings I speak of, inside every book in that store there was a solution, but of course only if you took the book seriously, as an instruction manual, you approached the book earnestly in order to fix some sort of wrong humans were befrought by, read it diligently from the beginning to the end and then followed precisely the recipes carefully measured out in its pages, step by step, not skipping a single step in order to get to the next step simply because the next step seemed more promising or more fitting to the lifting of the mood you were presently in, or because the mood you were in was in discord to the austere and un(com)promising manner that the present step called for. You simply did not find within yourself the power to overcome your debilitating impatience with the present step, you gave in to impatience, which the ancients railed against and many times even prohibited. And many of the books in the store were written or attributed to these superior ancients. So each and every step had to be executed and performed precisely according to the measurements and tallies prescribed in the book and you shouldn't complain if the plan held no promising results for you, no rewards in solving the problem you wished to solve and thus improve your life if you didn't follow precisely the book's prescriptions. You had no one to blame but yourself. I don't know if the visitors to the bookstore had the wherewithal to follow precisely the books' measurements—we're merely the chaff of the ancients, it has been suggested, or perhaps, as I at times see it, transmuting to new and unbearable formulations— or whether they would pick up one book which they never finished and then went back to the store hoping the next one they picked would hold for them more entrancing or easier to follow formulas for happiness and fulfillment, ones they could follow in a manner that was more fitting to personal inclination. Because there were so many formulas which were inclement to personal inclination, which, it may be stated here, were inimical, contemptuous even, of personal inclination, as though the world itself had been constructed thus, as a huge coliseum which had been doled out with general inclinations and the price of admission was your trading out your personal inclinations. These were all placed in a container and later that night admixed into the huge vat of general inclinations where they lost their unique flavor or taste but possibly left their minuscule imprint on the general, like a cappuccino sipped at a hoedown. Yes, perhaps many of those books were made up of formulas on how to relinquish gracefully your personal inclinations and maybe each of the customers—each one of them separately a splinter group, horrified at the insensitivity of the present— was a failed attempter in relinquishing personal inclinations, maybe each of the sleepwalking customers was a repeater, and thus an endless hoper, but still, I wasn't to judge them, you had to bow to them mainly for their endless and unceasing searching. So you could assume they came wishing to fix that fixation that clouded them, and that's why they came in. So entrancing was the bookstore in providing the atmosphere of the promise of problem solving, of wrong-correcting, that people crowded there every day and every night, somnambulating in silence through the mysterious vocabulary of its canopied alcoves, sectored by the tortuous labyrinth-like paths laid out by the crimson arrangement of the bookshelves, and lost and forgotten dreams like submerged symphonies wafted in this maze, mounted on the backs of the perpetual and therapeutic aromas and the burning incense. They came, they came, though many times they didn't know what precisely the wrong was that disrupted their idea of delightful being-in-the-world that they craved, but they knew there was one, the fixation that grounded them. Yes, they were the seekers, ignorers of Marx's dynamics. They came in droves, hoping they could walk in and end up picking the book containing the solution to the disrupting wrong. Many books in there were like that, but the people didn't know which one it was when they came in but they knew in their heart of hearts, incited by the incense and the wafting dreams, that one book like that was there when they came in. They floated about in silence, ashamed to look at others' eyes, a parade of women and men with long-hated fixations they hoped they could scrape off or wash or chase away. It was reported— yes there were those rare cases—that some even shed their fixations in the store, and the fixations, some even inherited from childhood, others from past lives even, hovered and wafted about like viruses in search of a new carrier and if you were not careful to conform to the dictates of certain unspoken and arcane prescriptions, a hated and troublesome—but maybe entrancing as well—fixation might attach itself to you unknowingly and you left the store suddenly possessed, in the grips of gestures and uncontrollable floccilations that embraced you firmly despite your previously held astrological charts or opposing Freudian dilemmas or Jungean unguents. *For we are mysteriously made thus, we are befrought with magnetisms that occur incessantly but we know nothing of, magnetisms whose functioning occurs of its own want and motivated by factors whose purposes may be at cross-purpose with our purposes.* Because how often do we spend our time sounding the call of our purposes? Sounding the summons of purposes? How many of us may hear those summons? Yet, they sound for all. All are summoned out of their habit formations, are summoned to disinhabit their self-imposed habit formations in which they march from horizon to concluded horizon, fumbling with the certainty of a moral certainty.

☿

As for me, I don't know what sort of wrongs those customers were flailing in the grip of. There are so many catalogues of wrongs I have no access to and which surprise me still when I hear of them in the consternation of a digesting voice at after-dinner, accompanied by perplexed gesticulations forcing my eyes to dart athwart. They didn't pause to consider that these fixations were the anthem of the summoning call. So they hovered about the store in silence, lost in the maze and glancing surreptitiously from the corners of their eyes at the bookshelves, hoping they could spot the bookshelf that stacked the books whose subject matter was in accord with the rubric they craved, unspotted by the severe judgment of the fellow fixators. She was wrapped tight in layered black and I recognized in her the possibility of a future wounding I adored, though I suspected that at times she was also a wounded volunteer in the practice of mercy. (But to take too easy a reading of *wounding* is not to collect the gift. It is the wounding, the wounding that you choreographed on the purpled living—it has taken me years to describe it—thus it is the wounding which I have gained. A wounding I cannot exhibit or sell, more expensive than if the entire intimacy of our adventures were to be found out. But, not to see our passage together as an illness, a societal disorder. Because perhaps, I intuited, she was a grave danger to society. No, not a single heart cocooned into the obscurity of its internal singular drama but a far larger farce lapping at the shore with the absolute. Perhaps I should have said she cast herself as a member of a distant and untouchable hierarchy of severity—rarely marketable—in whose baroque and beyond-the-horizon convolutions I was the unmistakable fog and I found myself aspired in a retiring post on the paths of her disapprovals. Despite all that, I presented myself as an imprecise impressario of vertigo, a fabricant of imprecision, and impiously bragged of the coruscating adagio for intestinal strings I was composing at the time.)

☿

There were bulbs there, though I don't remember them, there must have been, there must have been illumination in the Bodhi Tree, that's how we saw each other, it was late at night, it was after dark, to be precise, in any case, I could see her and she could see me, I assume she could see me, because though I write about her coat, if she had not showed up for future encounters, the meaning of our meeting might have been lost to memory, though I doubt it, but she showed up and continued so enough times that this writing, now, seven years later, is engendered, word by word, before your eyes. I engrave these words because I wish to be about her now and I wish to locate the specifics I wish to be about. Thus, place. There are these specifics, they are located inside a terrain within, a territory within, like a memory to which I have no access. This is of course a mere assumption based upon unexplored cultural assumptions, things I have heard from others, things in books I read, perhaps personal experiences. It seems as if I am reaching into the void in order to articulate it. I suppose that if I sit here and don't give in to amnesia or to impatience, a pathway to these stored details will open and access to the words containing these details will be opened and the words, demanding to be placed upon the screen before me, an intermediary stage before they get to the page, and your eyes, will use my fingers for such purpose. I wish to be about the border of word formation. I invoke the summoning of word formation, from these details stored in what is supposed to be called memory. Because if it is something that we forgot and that though it is in the nature of sloth and divinity to embrace forgetting like a curtain that falls endlessly over our doing, forgetting is also a defiance, a concealing before whose force we are helpless. Perhaps begging is a pathway, or at least praying might be appropriate here, an outright worship before the gates of forgetting, a summoning. Notice I am not speaking of forgetfulness, but of forgetting itself, placing it on a plinth, like a horseman in the city square, like a cross-fade into nothingness; into a conniving nothingness moreover, a pouch made of a material we don't understand, a material unavailable to our understanding, this understanding that returns each day at dawn, this understanding like a ticket without which entry to the daily forced march of habit formations is prohibited, but this pouch, unavailable to this understanding, like a great sleep, a pouch into which we are not allowed to peer, a pouch redefining peering for you or redefining you for peering, or peering redefining you. I said I placed forgetting on a plinth but I also said access to the words containing these details will be opened and the words, demanding to be placed upon the screen before me, an intermediary stage before they get to the page, will use my fingers for such purpose. This is of course if we assume that words are storage places for details, a fact I don't know. Were there words in the original universe or were they added later? Many have assumed much, much has been written, but is it the truth? If we assume that words are beasts of burden for meanings. Not merely "sounds unencumbered with precise meaning." That meanings hover about in the guise of words, that words cart meanings about, that words are the slaves of meanings, (do words court meanings? Do meanings court words?), and I don't mean this metaphorically. I mean allegorically. Don't think I don't know grammar, I do. I could look up the expert definition of each if I wanted to and correct it in the text, even call up some of my professor friends, Wolfgang for instance, but I don't, because unlike many of you who read this, I respect the realm of incomprehension, no more doctors of prohibitions for me. What I was saying is what if the words revolted and made meanings their slaves. Or simply discarded them to fend for themselves. The words hovering about meaninglessly. Or using meanings randomly, or in manners that disrespect, purposefully so, I suppose, the meanings meanings wished to preserve themselves in and thus preserved gad about. Suddenly a meaning desperate to find a word to represent it. A word encompassing a meaning too large for its breaches. To take half a meaning from a word. A word which abandons its previous meaning. Granaries of words. A silo of used words. Words that refuse meanings and choose to rest in meaninglessness. But choosing to rest in meaninglessness, they attract meanings which wander in meaninglessness without a word to stand in for them. Like adopting a child. A step-word. A step-meaning. The mating of a step-word with a step-meaning. The erotic cravings rampant across the territory of meaninglessness attempt at random to abduct words to make their own meanings presentable. To be at the border of meanings. Once the revolution comes, and words throw off the yoke of meanings imposed upon them by meanings, everyone will feel a lot better, and a lot freer. I say this because you're much better off paying attention to what I'm saying than paying a visit to your shrink—and paying for it too—who will do nothing but coat your meanings in a new set of meanings you can't unglue or untangle. Take it up with the words instead.

☿

In this—this train of thought is entrancing—man is merely a terrain for these age-long confrontations, man is not the controller. Man wants merely to eat, to sleep, to reproduce, man is not concerned or troubled by these concerns, and so the words and the meanings run loose according to their own wants, needs. The battles take place nearly unbeknownst to man. A few may teach it in college, but who listens? Man wants to go to restaurants and order food, that's the only thing words are good for for man. But I said nearly unbeknownst. In a place between forgetfulness and the frayed edges of memory—but the memory of the menu occupies fiercely the fore and only those flailing on the fjords of discontent may glimpse into the royal distance the battling concerns battling despite them. I speak as a reporter from the fjords, one battling forlorn between forgetfulness and the battle I spoke of. Do I want to be a spokesman for words and their function, or for that matter for details? It's not even a matter of my wanting it or not, I'm just there. I am not expressing preference as I spot on my eye-piece fashioned of the spokes of broken umbrella, the single spoke of a broken umbrella to be truthful, the words and the details, and I love them and I crave them and sometimes they choose me, as though I were a very beautiful woman. And then I like to speak about them. What else would I do? So, to speak.

⚥

She was wrapped tight in layered black, I said that, black like petroleum, materials I am at a loss now how to name, because I am ordered to name, to name with specific names known in the traffic of the trade of the sartorial, though now I am satisfied merely to have said, to have written sartorial, sartorial whose lapidary elegance leaps out of the page and enthralls me, but beyond, if I were forced to describe from the point of view of the specific demands of the sartorial thesaurus, I would have to invest myself, to respond to the call of an investigation whose coordinates I am in discomfort to approach, or I would have to engage the circumference of knowns of a Sartorial Hierodule, none of whom or which are available or known to me presently. Which sartorials in service of Utility make usage of such lapidary manner, they dispatch it, they dispatch you, in such lapidary fashion. Lapidary fascism. But wool, wool I suppose you could call it, or the memory of wool, more specific I cannot give you. Wool or something made of materials whose sources I have not investigated—I vaunt that I investigate the all from which all emerges—and if I were to do so I am afraid of the facts I would find, facts of international import, profits counted in the shadows, I will not go there, something made to resemble it, to resemble the memory of wool, from sources whose origins I have not excavated, or sounded, perhaps petroleum based sources. Her coat made of the sources of wars. For the memory of wool from which we engage in wars. Perhaps, unwittingly, it's what you meant, Hart Crane, like me lover of Whitman, when you prophetically said: "The Soul by naphta fledged into new reaches." It was a pre-war mid-January, mild mid-January 1996, perhaps February, the war as it is could not have been foreseen then, not by us, the war whose flames and humiliations we reflect our present hearts in, are now the statues to present our hearts' content to be placed in public places. Perhaps it is a timeless tale I attempt, but its incipience is in mid-January 1996. Its incipience is not mid-January 1996, but we have to begin somewhere. She wore a head shawl, and by that she was a desert warrior. It is thus she made herself a desert warrior. A danger to society. I pause here to note this age of convolutions, involucruous identities, seemings layered in imprecise horizons, horizon lines you wish to cross, revealing further horizons in layered hues dissolving into other layered hues, horizons in whose dissolving hues you might yearn to be abducted, and one becomes skilled in the fashioning of these electrifying abductors culled from shadowy historical sources—an imprecise science of history, imprecise research methods are necessary here—and plugged in to the gushing reservoirs of unspoken desire. Desire which still gushes and spills from the primordial, the snake we crave, despite all attempts to still it, to distill it and yoke it to the routes of commerce and trade. These are quick notes I jotted down, quick impressions, wide brush strokes. But here I am getting ahead, ahead of myself. I can't just leap into how she elicited in me, how she awoke me to the Hierodule within, within me that is. Hierodule, such a lapidary pronunciation. I want to go back and speak, I feel myself under the obligation to return to the materials. Because my purpose here is to excavate. Maybe I am in the employ of the Queen of Definitions and I wish to disobey her. Or maybe the other way around. To both obey and disobey by defining undefined places. Or by undefining defined places. Either way, there will be no glossing over, even if I am forced to return, time and time again. I remember reading that Nabokov, in researching his Lolita, went to the small town whose imaginary approximation he wanted to place her in, in order to make note of details he might use in his "painting" of it. Nabokov said so himself, he was already past 50 and his powers of concentration or observation were waning, so he said. His purpose was merely to present a gloss of details in which to flytrap his readers. A gloss in which some hare-brained but fastidious researcher of the future might dip in and thus prove—for what purpose?—that indeed, Nabokov's catalogue of details conforms to historical accuracy, to "the two whores of metaphysics, place and time," as Gherasim Luca called them. This is not my concern, I find it a fanfaronade, a pointless idiocy, though I too am past 50. Merely to ridicule the post-refuse of production, in whose presence one wishes not to be. Much as I semi-admire Nabokov. As I said I do not even know Sartor's Thesaurus—and I don't even think of Sartre here—nor will I familiarize myself with it, not purposefully so. And if I did, because it is not my purpose to gloss you with accuracies, (it would be merely for the entrancement with—and orientation by— the weaving of sounds and not what they represent in your utilities), especially if the accuracies do not entrance me or cause me to wish to be in their presence while describing them. Yes, to wish to be in their presence, to bathe in the invasive warmth infusion while I place one word after another in the hope of maintaining the presence, of maintaining it in time, for a time, the time I struggle to maintain this presence. And if I do not wish to be in their presence, the details of these materials of her dress, I wish to know why. I wish to excavate the why. Yet, I wish to excavate, I wish to linger over the materials, but I do not wish to pause there. But to pause there, perhaps to blacken the page with text, not merely so, not merely to make the page as black as her coat, tight at the waist perhaps, perhaps to linger along the black of her coat, perhaps thus to excavate, simply by lingering, precisely but negligently lingering, precisely by lingering to eventually excavate. "The scarcely audible, immured promise."

☿

What do I wish? I will go on and excavate what I wish. I have no hope that I will excavate what I wish. But I will go on, because "the imperative is, strictly, one of attempt." Perhaps it is only my mood that I have no hope. I must not jinx the attempt by saying "no hope." I will attempt. As I said, there was nothing glossy in her materials. Perhaps that is why there was nothing glossy in her materials. The gloss, like a clarinet weave or something form-fitting, would have dissolved me instantly, and it would have caused me to gloss over them as I fell senseless in a swoon, I confess, though I do not wish to, though I do have antecedents to validate me in recorded history, antecedents I admire and wish to emulate but do not recall momentarily. But I am forced to confess, voluptuary of masterful swoons. It was black, perhaps wool, perhaps artificial, result of petroleum excavation, and it was not the wool itself that functioned as the psychic quicksand, merely to place the wool on the present screen promotes no craved abduction, not even a mild drowning, merely a rejection like that of the quotidian. Rather the layering, the layering and the black, layered like desert dunes, like I said I am struggling with description as I have not available to me the tools of description the trade sartorial warriorix stabs you with unexpectedly in quotidian conversation and entrances, not even a black that gleams or reflects light but one in which you instantly disappear because it absorbs you past it, one of a zero albedo count, if I may resort to astronomy's denominations for my nominations—nomenclator I—and perhaps by plunging into this albedo count we might gain valuable information about the materials I am seeking information about, the albedo count can furnish information about the below-the-surface content materials that offer to gratify no instant expectations in ancient veils or peripety, no promising flight from the quotidian. The head shawl, no longer wool, perhaps the natural issue of worms, nature's factory of worms, cultivated worms, yes, but worms nonetheless, the unadorned nature fashioning its own adornment, worms for the further purpose of adornment, worms whose lives' purpose has been engaged to serve our—those who can write—need for adornment, who just like us have been engaged to serve purposes whose purpose they do not comprehend, worms who just like us have been herded into the serving of purposes beyond our own purposes, indifferent of our own purposes, indifferent to their purposes, but the head shawl, whose purpose was to entrance me for who knows what further purpose, and by whom, outlining the circumference of your skull whose circumference I am suddenly gripped by a need to encircle, now, seven years later, the tips of my fingers presently leave the keyboard to encircle the imprecise memory of your skull's circumference, I wish to place my palms about its circumference, my palms whose fingers are presently lifting off the keyboard to encircle your skull's circumference, to grasp it between them, the roundness of it, an aesthetic pleasure I can't deny, but to attempt to describe it as round, or as oval is not called for, perfectly ovaloid, sphere, and all that I am left with is to lower my fingers in defeat back on the keys, perhaps to speak about it, which I don't know how, because how else can I encircle it except through the words which are presently blackening the page, and yet if I were to do so what vocabulary would I need, what dictionary use, how measure? there is a shape my finger-tipped, my palm's skin craves to touch, to feel its rounded contours, even to say this much I am struggling, but struggling to remain in your presence, Layson, struggling to recall the shape of your skull in order to affix it here on this page in order to keep it in my presence a little longer, for a long time, I long for it, because, and I am losing it and I have to at least cling to the head shawl before the winds of the Great Forgetfulness, or the Great Refusal, but the shawl, layered like desert dunes superimposed upon each other to entrance in advanced mysteries, and furrowed by tiny furrows that, if you were forced to investigate under the light of an inquiring force, you might trope to the tiny crumpled crease behind the longed for knee of the entrancing silk, or silk-like petroleum products, the vertigo promised by rumpling crease that abducts to beyonds beyond speaking descriptions, because once one is abducted one is beyond any attempt to describe, even the most intransigent flail here and succumb to the vertigo. There are of course writers about whom I have heard it said that they excel at description, who would have said simply that she wore a head shawl and name the material of the head shawl as it is commonly denominated in the world of finance and trade. The denuded of meaning material, denuded of travel routes and trade routes, denuded of veils and dreams. Its name must not be, under the pain of death, the utility's single monikered solution. The name must include the worm and its dreams, Kant's philosophy of the natural versus the artificial—"the imagination is a powerful agent of creation, a second nature out of the material supplied to it by actual nature. The material can be borrowed by us from nature... but be worked by us into something else"—must include the name of all those who wore it in all its guises, in all its incarnations, must include for certain the farmers' names and the sailors' names and the captain's name, all the sailors and all the captains and all the ship names. Must include all the thoughts of the women and the mirrors that showed them, the fluttered handkerchiefs on the harbor, the roses dropped in expectation, the fragrance of the afternoons in the tropics, and what the mirrors thought and what the worms thought and the roses. The name must be longer than a book and last at least twice as long to do it improbable justice. It must include the name of the describers, and those who did and those who did not succumb to the summons of the circumstance.

☿

Yes, I challenge you to find one who won't, one intransigent describer, one so skilled in the arts of indifference, one who will not, willingly, give up speaking, giving up the desire to speak, and succumb to the summons of that circumstance. Genius music is absent from one's desires, we were warned. Genius music may be absent by our desires. Because her scarf was an aroma before whose therapy I was powerless to hesitate, though what she abducted was beyond my knowledge to discern at that particular instant and in defense against this abduction I had craved, in order to subvert perhaps the lurking possibility of a subsequent disenchantment, I quickly relegated it to a veneer of the ironical quotidian with which I had coated myself with the passage of the years and whose faint veil I wielded in its approximate and quotidian denomination as charm, charm whose force, I should confess, I could never reliably rely on, rally at need, or even summon at will. Perhaps the central committee of my conviction's manufacturing companies was infused with Apathy, across a landscape that oozed Refusal. But the landscape she radiated with its umbilicus feeding off palaces from A Thousand and One Nights, baldachined bedrooms of Baudelairean intrigue, withdrew me into the veils of its vast horizons and porticoes of somnambulist peripety, and she galloped away, villainously. This is, of course, confession. But a double-edged confession, whose double edge you must grasp. Without it you are merely quotidian. I am returning, like I promised I would, because villainously made me think of velvet's villous and slow-motion somnambulism, but there was nothing there in what she wore apparently of sleep's villous black, nothing of that, her abduction into sleep was more audacious, her horizons of an apparently rougher cloth, though clearly not agrarian. An agrarian appeared later on—then vanished, all is sand—but not then and of another essence. More of that later, I promise, because we must perform a thorough sounding, I am resolutely committed to the thoroughness of the sounding I wish to perform. Unless of course I become bored and abandon the text's tedium. But there was no suspicion even of agrarian then. What is the use of saying then? Because to perform the sounding I wish to perform with the resoluteness I wish to perform it with I must excavate within the time frame that my memory provides me with. I must place my memory, no, I must subject my memory to a sound sounding, against the Great Refusal, against the suck of the Great Forgetfulness. Or even the Great Dispersal. Perhaps for this the future generations will speak of me. They will speak of one man's, of a man alone, on his excavating journey. What he has excavated, I do not know. But do not assume Freud found it all, do not be yoked to Jung. There are horizons they couldn't even hope for. This is merely the journey, and I may remind them the journey is all, embarking upon it, that is. I may flail, I will not fail. What was then the blaze of this material's essential fire? Am I perhaps looking in the mistaken direction, misdirection, am I missing the direction, to give such weight to the materials and none to the fire they shrouded? I am accused of this, as I am accused of entrancement with trivia, with trinkets. I am not a member of the voracious nations of history, I am not even from around here. Still, despite the accusation, I ignore it for now, endure it, though against its umbrage I shift in my sounding and may return to its summons, I will return, it is the materials I wish to pursue, perhaps the albedo count may give us a clue, or perhaps I am not capable presently of describing this fire that inhabited the materials, perhaps I am fearful, perhaps it gleamed too much brilliance, more than I am willing to ignite presently. Light too is a material, yet we only capture it by making materials that reflect it. We could never use it to dress up in, we merely masquerade, marionettes of the sun king, in cheap materials obtained from the sweat of the hoi-polloi, that we have invested with market variety of chattoyancy. *But perhaps they merely shame you into materials because the possibility you might become light frightens them.* Ah, but to wrap your confreres in the skin of delight!

The evanescent gold of the phantasy inhabits the corpse.

⚥

Perhaps it was only in my native formulations that I clung to a congenital comfort, of the villiousness of velvet, a quicksand of silk and shrunk before the lack of albedo count and before its implication of nettlesome stab. This I will speak of later. But when she galloped off she had abducted, we were in Los Angeles, in California, whose desert had never left, whose Fata Morganas were still the rule, what had been built atop it merely to serve them, these Phantasmic Hashishin Assassinas of which she was one, I am indulging here perhaps in a romantic notion of what she might have been, which I'm not sure is not veiling what I am attempting to unveil, and in doing so I am not convinced this is not the ruse of the Great Forgetfulness, whose armies are the purpose of the Great Refusal, the intransigent purpose, prose, of the Great Refusal, though in doing so I am perhaps approaching an aspect of the truth, the truth that I am seeking of her being, of my being, of our being together for the time we were together, of the implied promise of our being together, suddenly I could say, at least for now, I could be wrong should I be forced to confine myself to a definite definition, but for a moment, a diaphanous ephemera, I could define her fire, again I speak of seeking definitions, but seeking only, always seeking, never pausing to define, in a state of perpetual never-pausing-to-define, and the seeking is the fire, and I venture here to define that her fire was made of Sleep, of a kind of Sleep, you notice I invoke the capital S to evoke not only the sleep of a night but an Ur-Sleep if I may but please forgive me, not Sleep itself but a kind of Sleep, Sleep as a way of being, Sleep as a denial of Utility, a Sleep that envelopes all your formulations, there is nothing of you not enveloped in Sleep, as though the bottom of the sea surrounded you and your perambulating about in your utility were merely of an immaterial seam, an immaterial seeming, Sleep with all its loopholes and whirlwinds and veils, I am not here writing copy for Sleep, it is not a place to visit and vacation in in order to renew yourself for the purposes of Utility, her hair was Sleep, with its soft amber-sounding strands, but I am not there yet, I don't wish to deviate from the path of definitions I had begun a few sentences earlier, the Fata Morganas she was serving, we're traversing perhaps the same territory here as sleep, Sleep, she was perhaps in service perhaps to another more powerful, perhaps the Queen, no, Empress Califa herself, maybe an emanation of her, I am merely guessing, whose sleep was this land we inhabited, I wrote territory rather than land earlier but soon caught myself and realized I didn't want any *rs* in Sleep, the Empress whose name, despite the betrayal, still veiled this land, invests this land, is the unfathomable being animating this land, whose somnambulist aroma we were so mad to inhale. Speaking of soul, animating is of an accord I presently and momentarily agree with. Yes, it was wool, a wool whose zero count albedo convolutions abducted me, of whose absorbing aroma I was mad to inhale and she galloped away and I was gone. I could speak, I should speak of the wrappings contouring her lower limbs too, I wanted to say legs but it was too quotidian, though lower limbs too does not live up to the enrapturing, nothing does, no word presents itself that corresponds, enrapturing, yes, I should address that enrapturing, I want to address it, enwrapturing, I want to be there, but not yet, duty says I want to address what exactly she abducted. Though to renounce, even momentarily, the description, to renounce a description, of how her legs were enwrapped, and the

resulting accented contours, is a difficult task, like that of an acolyte, a
catechumen ascetic having received his first assignment, to renounce
the thought, to renounce even the thought, to renounce indulging
in the thought, even momentarily, to enthusiastically take instant
action to impede self from ever indulging, even in the thought, of
ever touching a lover, ever again, one forced by the exactness of calling
to tear, wrench, from the surface of soul any remains of attachment
to longing, and find the comfort he sought in the Supreme Being,
whose future he now suddenly doubts, whose name he now with
horror apprehends is none other than the Feared, the Horrific, the
Great Consoling Blank. The legs revealed, I lose, the convent was
never for me, I am succumbing to the summons of their maternal
enwrapturing trance, to the call of their beyond, and the powers of
description, which I have never in any case claimed to be a master
of, have been momentarily suspended. Perhaps this confession buys
me some time for the present because surely I will return, perhaps
I am strengthened and invigorated merely by the thought of their
presence, by my defeat, a capitulation of wet defeat before their
commanding significance. As I fall on the field, but by no means as
a Freudian desperado. So I will return, now I want return to, I want
to speak of what exactly she abducted but again, here too, I find it
impossible to do so. I am flailing again before an imponderable as
I do, as I attempt to speak of what she abducted, what exactly did
she abduct, from the secret fabric of my formulations, something
negligible, a faint wisp of a sine-qua-non you neglect until it is
gone, a weave the thinness of a negligee, certainly you will blame
me for succumbing to naming it a negligee, by that naming, first,
causing your fingertips to join together as though to grasp for the
purposes of stroking for the purposes of obtaining a secret pleasure,
a titillation even I might venture to declare, call me a titillitarian,
to confess, not as a Freudian desperado, and second, to falling for
precision when the imprecise is summoning, especially these days,
this era of dreams of empires when the imprecise is neglected, when

the force of an entire industry is engaged in suppressing the imprecise, neglecting the imprecise, or suppressing by neglect, but, this occurs to me now, should a prophet of the imprecise, a Prophet of the Imprecise rise and rouse the masses to rise to levels of imprecision, these days of empire dreams, rise to levels of calculation denials, become practitioners of imprecision and denials of calculations, where they take on a daily and strict practice of imprecision, of denial of calculations, alone or in groups, forming neighborhood groups, churches even, en masse, a critical mass I say, would they not engage the National Guard, the military even, yes, the military too, to quell it, but is it not true that the military is engaged in the service of suppression of the imprecise, this is how far this has now gone, the military too is engaged in the suppression of the imprecise, it's come to this, with its own police and army and informers of definers of precision to hold the public in the precise thrall of its definitions, to imprison the public in the fly-trap of definitions, from which there is no escape and perhaps only the flailing in its grip and the ensuing forgetfulness might transmute to a new and powerful imprecision to rescue and redeem us, the great hope, but for now, now, negligee, naming it negligee, after negligible and neglect, and how many of us could proudly declare before the Ultimate Tribunal, could brag of a lifespan devoted to excavating neglect to the extent of placing it lovingly, or negligibly, enthusiastically on a rostrum, no, more, an altar, loving it and worshiping it more than art itself, making neglect into art, taking neglect and placing on a rostrum with such purposeful worship, infusing it with such purposeful worship that it becomes art, art of the masses, everyone becomes an artist of excavating neglect, it is all anyone desires and spends any time in pursuit of, taking all preciousness down from the altar, though this has already occurred, probably,

but for our present purposes,

naming it negligee and then to fixing it to a definite island, however imprecise this island, it was so obvious a connection, so devious, like something you wish to put on that you shouldn't, like a secret you wish to mask myself in, which you adore but only the veil of its imprecision do you mask myself in, but this island, enough to injure the idea of the imprecise, still I am not far from wrong (or right) in describing it thus, she filched this something in all seriousness from my, from a subtle interior weave inside my formulations, inside of how I am formulated inside, though the Great Refusal would deny that the material of the immaterial negligee exists, that Great Refusal that consumes this faint wisp of texture that forms these formulations that give significance to the daily flailing, the drear of weeks, I am recapturing it now, the faint weave that infuses the drear of weeks with the texture of significance. Maybe I am just merely blackening the pages with text, but as black as what she veiled her fire of sleep in. Maybe, like a child at play, a child of sleep, I am unraveling her coat, her black coat strand by strand, against someone's wishes, and deriving the guilty pleasure assigned to such tasks and the desire for the punishment of guilt. Maybe it was only a strand from this negligible negligee that she took, because she probably realized I was a willing hierodule in her temple then, had been a prodigal hierodule, but was repentant and willing and ready to return, and she abducted this strand as a tease, a tantalizing taunt, knowing I would follow anywhere either to recapture, to beg for it that it be returned, or, more, to grant her the remains. How could her wool coat and headscarf subjugate thus? Was it by the summons of the Sleep's fire? And the promise of the contour, of course, that I haven't yet spoken of. I coated myself, shortly upon her exit, as I mentioned, as post facto defense, in a veneer of the ironical, the corner of my upper lip skywise as I studied from a sequence of childhood's cinematographical statues in stances against the Destinal. I had coated myself with quotidian against the Destinal, denying the summons I had a lifetime prepared for in-nocturnal journeys to the region surrounding the Unfathomble, habitually concealing my falling from slow towers on full moon nights cloaked by the clouds of the Illumined. Why, a declared traveler to the Unfahomable as myself, doomed to the vice of the Unfathomable, refuse the summons, perhaps the Destinal Summons, Summons for which I had so long long studied, of perhaps the Empress, Empress Califa herself, whose Hierodule I had studied to have been each night. I was chosen, the Chosen. Why coat myself with this veneer of irony against the predestinal journey?

☿

Night was stalking at the fringe of your collar
Night the essence of fright and reckoning
Night the incessant tincture of wind and concealment
Night of coming to be and never yet here vanquished
Night the essence of the final invasion
Night Mother of wefts of abduction
The intersticing pearls of sunburn and forgiving
Night the final revelation
Night of next door screams in the night
Now here

☿

I am returning again to her costume. I am not satisfied at all with the description I made of her clothes, especially the top, which I don't remember. All that remains is something indefinite, which I wish to define. But so that it remains as indefinite as it has remained. Because it has remained, and this is notable. I can note here what she wore not, what her costume was not. It was not a man's jacket. But perhaps it had been fashioned from one, the male refashioned, merely to mock the male. I wear the male so well yet I am not one. I am a man she said later, trapped in this female body. Am I forced now to go looking through these fashion magazines arraying the racks in the hope of finding the one article that might approximate for me what she wore? Simply to find a word, the right describing word? Because this is not about finding the right word to cause you the flash of insight into the material her coat that I am speaking of was made of. It is not about that at all. It is about spending time with the coat, and the coat was, around the coat, or rather around the forgetfulness of it, in speaking of it, causing the lingering around it. Yet spending time lingering is plinking one key after the next on my iBook's keyboarded letters to form one word after the next. Yet the call of the word is inevitable, incessant. The call for leaving behind the keyboarded instrument, but just to write instrument, I don't know what I am doing to this text, I am causing a run in the clarinet causing this text, this text, I don't know what instrument does to the texture of the text and I am furious that I used it and suspicious of it. And it is too late now. But to leave behind the texture of the text in search of a word that will enhance it, in search of a word that will continue it, to deem suddenly to walk out the door, to venture my two legs forward, journey forth. But I don't even know where to look, should I start in the fashion section at Borders? If I did so, I would have to do so surreptitiously. I would have to resort to my reservoirs of the surreptitious. I have many of those. Those I have found, in passing merely, the surreptitious to be unreliable as a source of, through merely to say the surreptitious, but I said in passing merely. Still I cannot help in wishing to brush against the surreptitious, to embrace it, not publicly, but it is not even a matter of that, of course not publicly, to coat myself in the surreptitious like a thick juice, like a case of paresthesia, because from what rostrums would you preach in favor of its mass consumption, how do you feed the public the surreptitious, or I should say, how do you feed them on the surreptitious, or with it, like a secret happiness to nourish on. But I said in passing. Still, it is surreptitiously that I cling to the coat and to the fabric of the coat and going against its zero albedo count whose wish is to swallow me, though I cannot be allowed to be swallowed inside this zero albedo count like a black hole.

☿

Perhaps I fear its obliteration. Perhaps I fear obliteration. Or prefer it. Perhaps I don't see anything in it. Or perhaps a faceless general black I can't describe holds no entrancing more for me. A disappearance I fear and I am left borderless without my surreptition. Perhaps I do not know how to transcend the zero albedo count. Perhaps it is not the longed-for "nocturnal depth of subjectivity". The expected unexpected "aux millieu des ombres fantastiques". Perhaps this is the symphony of my wounded shoestrings. Perhaps the Great Dispersal. Perhaps I do not see how be swallowed in mere glitterless black, mere glitterless is not entrancing, perhaps my congenital progress towards wanton obliteration via the vibratory ciliae of frottage is the cause, meandering congenital ciliae. My only, only resistance against obliteration, a putsch perhaps against it. Holding on against it by the glittering of the minuscule ciliae. Because even a minuscule glimmer which, I am hanging on a word here, in questioning its origin, and by that I am questioning the origin of all minuscule glimmers because the specific stands in for the general, it is said, but it is far better, this minuscule glimmer can only have originated in the thin filament that delicate spiders nourished on concepts of luminosity embroidered on her coat. The glimmer remains unobstructed in its abstraction; the abstraction remains unobstructed in memory; and one should ask, one is impelled to probe into the malady of memory, into the remorseful islands infused of a forced glimmer; because she moved, as it is to be expected, all of us by nature of being incessantly move, it is an attribute of our being that we move, that we are in constant motion, in our march, mostly forced, solitary or not, through the world, though much of it is spent in standing, not stepping forth, not marching, but facing one another or each other in exchanges of utterings, *that is how our fate as a species at this moment in time has positioned us* and none has probed into the Being's purpose for positioning us thus, so near the statuary are we, such habit formations, so ungraspable to our lips, our throats stutter in pure unuttering to define the malady of our forced positions, while the rest of us fumbles in forgetfulness, we don't know, we don't know! and so positioned our movements are minuscule when compared to, say, the frog's leaping, the ballerina's gargouillade, or the sword arm raised, then lowered, and thus extinguishing being. But perhaps not Being. (All this perhaps because we mostly meet inside and even when we meet in open air, it is not the "open air" the poet speaks of: "Here a great personal deed has room/such a deed seizes upon the whole race of men/its effusion of strength and will overwhelms law and mocks all authority and all argument against it". But our open air is the shopping malls, that's now the open road the poet speaks of.) Still despite the minuscule motion I spoke of, the glimmer itself must not have endured longer than the instant it took for millimeter length swivel contributed by your body during which the bulbs' light reflected in the (gl)amorous grammar of the filament. The glimmer a new development. There was probably more than one filament embroidered—embroidered is too intrusive a word—sewn in the surface of the fabric of the coat, thus the zero albedo count of which I spoke earlier was in fact counterpointed by a millimeter redemption from the rostrum accusing it of nothing but such quality of light, obliterate of consciousness.

☿

In doing so, in so seeking, seeking to continue blackening the pages with text, you go against the Great Refusal, you raise a flailing arm against the Great Refusal, an intransigent void that sucks memories, and you must unravel the texture strand by strand, patiently, penitently, strand by strand, exercising the paramita of patience, patience and penitence, not ignoring the slightest of stitch, returning again and time again to the most unpromising of strands, uncompromisingly stitch by unpromising stitch. Her clothes with their suggestion of meandering labyrinths, with their many folds, pliès, with their implications, applications, the plight of the unwitting traveler, such as you, plication. Implication of the text in the layering, plié, implied complication, the plight. You are blackening the pages with text, with meandering paths where the plight of the unwitting traveler is implicated in concealing folds, in the layering of the plié, in the implication, in plication. You are in the shadows, but like the man said, "the shadow in the end is no better than the substance."

☿

Certainly I am not bringing charges against you for the shape of the coat, oh you who animated that coat, it was the animator I wanted, the manipulator of the mask you made, this mask against whose material I rail, a material whose concealed defense I am carrying. (But to say clothed, to say unclothed, is it not merely to imagine the what-ifs of a subserved mentality? Is it not merely to fanfaroon for industries of precision?). Which part of what she wore led to the promises of bedrooms and what sort of bedrooms were they? Were you seeking the one upon whom you would confer your ultimate premium, "the Brahman who understood my proverbs"? This question implied, sooner or later. It is a daring question, one opening paths, but this is what you must perhaps ask. Not now, later. Or now. The question itself is a path, it has been said.

☿

Certainly the insinuation that issued from you, you the manipulator of the mask, in service of, as I later saw, procreation, but, as it turned out, not the procreation of what you overtly stated you had targeted and had practiced for, of this I will speak later, of this I hope to speak later but who knows, you became despite yourself the andro-procreator, of this text, now parading disobediently before your eyes, presently parading because you infused, me, your actions like a positor deposited in me the need to make this text whose texture you are befuddled by or delighting in presently, this text I now despair you will not read, this text others but not you will speak of me for, this insinuation you deposited, this issue of an insinuation whose tension I am attempting to detail in this reportage of its reticulating venation of cross-purposes in retrospect, the issue of this insinuation which you manipulated with what you were vested with in the Bodhi Tree, a battle whose reticulatory cross-purposing tensions I find presently valuable to meander in for revelatory sport.

☿

A waist coat, I suppose, but akin to a primordial tunic represented in the pages of the time before time, or a distant double, disobedient of the strict tracks of time, of the doublet, male array made double amorous by the purposeful smuggling across the gender-tracks but proposing across the centuries a disobedient positing of the male, proposing possibilities for futures of gender disobedience. Perhaps we were the spokes, the spokesmen and women, at the hub of a future of cross-gendering, a future of unspoken nocturnal luxuries.

☿

The layering, Layson, yes, the layering of the folds of the head scarf like desert dunes, to abduct like a galloping desert warrior whose purpose is to transport, but without the gravity of gravity, where your balance was at risk but engendered by desire alone, more, by the keen uniqueness of unrepentable and unrepeatable desire and the gravity was a punishment issued to those whose listening to the dictates of this desire was imprecise in according to its strict formulations; and each time a Freudian Generalissimo was at attention to catalogue for publication and prohibition. Oh Layson!

You placed me as you flailed in the grips of galloping but more you will not reveal, not for shame but so as not to elicit from a Freudian Generallisimo an illicit public issue.

☿

Because this clarinet, this imponderable clarinet, instead of being a material bordering, a thin material bordering this and that, even who and what perhaps, and measuring high on the scintillation counter, a complete and maternal enveloping presentness whose albedo count is one, this complete enveloping presentness which I assume into my own existence, the clarinets must be measured by the flux density of radiant energy per unit they emit, and here I must admonish myself for measuring that which should not be measured, but then I always balance on the borders of prohibitions, I must admonish myself (but also applaud myself) for speaking the unspeakable, the unspeakable vice, and I am sorry, I will write the Unspeakable with a capital U, this clarinet, because if I say clarinet—and as I wrote clarinet, the clarinet part from Messaien's *Quatuor pour la Fin du Temps' Louange a l'Eternite de Jesus* was just playing (the concatenation of Jesus and clarinet makes me wonder what Jesus would have thought—I live in the South—of my affliction with the surreptitious clarinets), and if you don't know it, or have it, rush to your nearest Borders to get it—but I was speaking of the borders of this to that and in-between this immaterial clarinet, this thin nothingness longing, scintillating the bordering between the this and the that, yes if I say clarinet, I am merely entertaining myself, tooting the strands of a wind from the beyond on my *néant* clarinet, a *néant* wind for myself alone with no claims to traversing the treacherous straights on the way to the creaky podium of world literature. A mere solo wind on the clarinet of nothingness and to last me just as long.

Julian Semilian is a filmmaker, novelist and poet. Born in Romania, he has edited numerous features during a long Hollywood career and is a Professor of film editing and experimental and documentary cinema at the University of North Carolina School of the Arts. His experimental and documentary projects have been screened and exhibited at galleries, museums and festivals, both nationally and internationally.

JULIANSEMILIAN.COM

BLACK WIDOW PRESS MODERN POETS

All the Good Hiding Places by Ralph Adamo

ABC of Translation by Willis Barnstone

The Secret Brain: Selected Poems 1995-2012 by Dave Brinks

Caveat Onus: The Complete Poem Cycle by Dave Brinks

Forgiven Submarine by Andrei Codrescu and Ruxandra Cesereanu

Crusader Woman by Ruxandra Cesereanu

Too Late for Nightmares by Andrei Codrescu

Anticline by Clayton Eshleman

Archaic Design by Clayton Eshleman

Alchemist with One Eye on Fire by Clayton Eshleman

The Price of Experience by Clayton Eshleman

Pollen Aria by Clayton Eshleman

The Essential Poetry (1960 to 2015) by Clayton Eshleman

Grindstone of Rapport: A Clayton Eshleman Reader by Clayton Eshelman

Penetralia by Clayton Eshleman

Clayton Eshleman: The Whole Art Edited by Stuart Kendall

Barzakh (Poems 2000-2012) by Pierre Joris

Packing Light: New & Selected Poems by Marilyn Kallet

How Our Bodies Learned by Marilyn Kallet

The Love That Moves Me by Marilyn Kallet

The Hexagon by Robert Kelly

Fire Exit by Robert Kelly

Garage Elegies by Stephen Kessler

BLACK WIDOW PRESS
POETRY IN TRANSLATION

Exile Is My Trade: A Habib Tengour Reader by Habib Tengour. Translated by Pierre Joris

Present Tense of The World: Poems 2000-2009 by Amina Said. Translated by Marilyn Hacker

Endure: Poems by Bei Dao. Translated by Clayton Eshleman and Lucas Klein

Curdled Skulls: Poems of Bernard Bador by Bernard Bador. Co-translated and edited by Clayton Eshleman

Pierre Reverdy: Poems Early to Late by Pierre Reverdy. Translated by Mary Ann Caws and Patricia Terry

Selected Prose and Poetry of Jules Supervielle by Jules Supervielle. Translated by Nancy Kline, Patrica Terry, and Kathleen Micklow

Poems of Consummation by Vicente Aleixandre. Translated by Stephen Kessler

A Life of Poems, Poems of a Life by Anna de Noailles. Translated by Norman R. Shapiro

Furor & Mystery and Other Poems by Rene Char. Translated by Mary Ann Caws and Nancy Kline

The Big Game (Le grand jeu) by Benjamin Péret. Translated by Marilyn Kallet

Essential Poems & Prose of Jules Laforgue by Jules Laforgue. Translated by Patricia Terry

Preversities: A Jacques Prevert Sampler by Jacques Prevert. Translated by Norman R. Shapiro

La Fontaine's Bawdy by Jean de la Fontaine. Translated by Norman R. Shapiro & Illustrated by David Schorr

Inventor of Love by Gherasim Luca. Translated by Julian and Laura Semilian

Art Poetique by Guillevic. Translated by Maureen Smith with Lucie Albertini Guillevic

To Speak, to Tell You? by Sabine Sicaud. Translated by Norman R. Shapiro

Poems of A. O. Barnabooth by Valery Larbaud. Translated by Ron Padgett and Bill Zavatsky

EyeSeas (Les Ziaux) by Raymond Queneau.

Translated by Daniela Hurezanu and Stephen Kessler

Essential Poems and Writings of Joyce Mansour by Joyce Mansour. Translated by Serge Gavronsky

Essential Poems and Writings of Robert Desnos:
A Bilingual Anthology by Robert Desnos.
Translated by Mary Ann Caws, Terry Hale, Bill Zavatsky, Martin Sorrell, Jonathan Eburne, Katherine Connelly, Patricia Terry, and Paul Auster

The Sea and Other Poems (1977-1997) by Guillevic.
Translated by Patricia Terry "Jerry

Love, poetry, (L'Amour La Poesie, 1929) by Paul Eluard.
Translated by Stuart Kendall

Capital of Pain by Paul Eluard.
Translated by Mary Ann Caws, Patricia Terry, and Nancy Kline

Poems of André Breton, A Bilingual Anthology.
Translated by Jean-Pierre Cauvin and Mary Ann Caws

Last Love Poems of Paul Eluard
Translated by Marilyn Kallet

Approximate Man' & Other Writings by Tristan Tzara.
Translated by Mary Ann Caws

Chanson Dada: Selected Poems of Tristan Tzara.
Translated by Lee Harwood

Disenchanted City: La ville désenchantée by Chantel Bizzini.
Translated by Marilyn Kallet and J. Bradford Anderson

Guarding the Air: Selected Poems of Gunnar Harding.
Translated by Roger Greenwald

BLACK WIDOW PRESS BIOGRAPHY

Revolution of the Mind: The Life of Andre Breton by Mark Polizzotti

WWW.BLACKWIDOWPRESS.COM